The rumors are flying
at Bayside High!

Mary-Kate and Ashley
Sweet 16

Keeping Secrets

By Melinda Metz

📽HarperEntertainment
An Imprint of HarperCollins*Publishers*

A PARACHUTE PRESS BOOK

A PARACHUTE PRESS BOOK

Parachute Publishing, L.L.C.
156 Fifth Avenue, Suite 302
New York, NY 10010

Published by
HarperEntertainment
An Imprint of HarperCollins*Publishers*
10 East 53rd Street, New York, NY 10022-5299

SWEET 16 books are created and produced by Parachute Press, L.L.C., in cooperation with Dualstar Publications, a division of Dualstar Entertainment Group, LLC., published by HarperEntertainment, an imprint of HarperCollins Publishers.

ISBN 0-06-055645-5

First printing: August 2003

Printed in the United States of America

Visit HarperEntertainment on the World Wide Web at
www.harpercollins.com

10 9 8 7 6 5 4 3 2 1

chapter one

I opened the door to the girls' bathroom. The smell of powder, deodorant, and hair gel tickled my nose. I sneezed.

"Ashley, come over here for a second," Alicia Gorman whispered.

I glanced around. There was no one else in the bathroom, so why was she whispering? I shrugged and walked over to her.

Alicia didn't look at me. She just kept staring at herself in the mirror hanging over the sink at the end of the row.

"Do you think it's true?" Alicia asked, still whispering.

"Do I think what is true?" I asked.

Alicia shook her head. "Sorry," she said. She was finally talking in regular volume. "It's stupid,

I know. I shouldn't even be thinking about it."

She took a deep breath. "You don't think I have a . . . a face that only a pug dog could love, do you?"

"What are you talking about?" I asked.

Alicia tapped her button nose. "Because of this. Because it's squashy."

"Of course not!" I said. "Your nose is adorable. Why would you even think something like that?"

Alicia waved her hands helplessly in front of her face. "Just something someone said. Are you sure? You don't think I need a nose job?"

"A nose job!" I cried. "You must be kidding. Isn't that a little drastic?"

She frowned. "I guess you're right. Thanks, Ash. See you in English."

She adjusted her big rhinestone USA belt buckle. Then she straightened her shoulders and marched out of the bathroom.

Well, that was weird, I thought to myself as I slipped into the nearest stall. I hung my purse on the metal hook on the back of the door.

A few moments later, the bathroom door slammed and I heard giggling as a couple of girls came into the bathroom.

"Yeah, I totally agree," a girl said. I didn't recognize her voice. "Teena McGuire is absolutely one hundred percent beast. She's never had a boyfriend in her entire life!"

Did I hear that right? I knew Teena. She was a sweet girl. Why would anyone call her a beast?

I grabbed my purse and left the stall, but no one was at the row of sinks. I didn't get to see who was gossiping about Teena.

I flew through the hallways to the main entrance. Brittany Bowen and Lauren Glazer, two of my best friends, were waiting for me there.

"Hey, guys!" I called. "No Mary-Kate yet?"

They shook their heads.

The four of us always like to meet up early on Thursday mornings. It's never too soon to start planning for the weekend!

"She had to pick up something from her desk at the school Website office," I said. "She should be here any second."

"And what's *your* excuse for being late?" Brittany pretended to be annoyed. She adjusted the sparkly clips in her curly black hair and admired the effect in her mirror.

"Bathroom stop," I said. "You won't believe what I heard in there. Two girls were talking. I didn't recognize the voices. But they called Teena

McGuire a complete beast! Isn't that awful?"

Lauren's blue eyes widened in outrage. "That's so mean!"

Brittany shook her head. "This school has turned into gossip central."

"What do you mean?" I asked.

"Look around." Brittany flung her arms out wide.

I glanced around the hallway. It was more crowded than it usually was this early in the morning. Groups of kids stood around chatting instead of heading off to class.

Hillary Berg and Gretchen Patterson—both in their cheerleading uniforms—stood close together a few feet away from us. A spirit banner hung limply between them, its end trailing on the floor. Kids were stepping on it, but the two girls didn't notice. They were too busy whispering to each other.

Gretchen glanced back at the girl, who flashed her a pleading look. But Gretchen only smirked, turned back to Hillary, and whispered some more.

Another cheerleader I didn't know glared at Hillary and Gretchen from her spot over by the drinking fountain. She twirled her long ponytail around and around. She did not look happy.

Bill, a guy I knew from English class, was leaning against another guy's locker. They were both looking at the girl by the drinking fountain and whispering. Then they started laughing so hard they couldn't talk.

"You're right," I answered. "It's like there's a big game of telephone going on."

I dropped my backpack on the floor and sat down on the padded bench outside the administration office. Brittany and Lauren sat down next to me.

"I wonder what everyone is talking about—a big secret or some juicy gossip?" Lauren said. "I know it's absolutely none of my business, but now I'm curious."

"I'm not." Brittany frowned at a speck of gum on the cork sole of one of her chunky sandals. "Most gossip isn't worth the time it takes to listen to."

I pulled a tissue out of my backpack and handed it to Brittany.

"Thanks, Ashley," she said.

I smiled at her and pulled out the accordion file I use for Love Link paperwork. There was an application for my matchmaking service on the school Website that I wanted to go over before the bell rang.

"How's traffic on the Love Link site?" Brittany asked, eyeing the Love Link sticker on my file folder.

"Bumper to bumper," I joked as I ran my finger down the application. All the info was filled in—favorite things, hobbies, and interests.

"I checked out the site last night. It's getting huge!"

Lauren said. "I can't believe how many new people signed up."

"You're not thinking of trading in Ben, are you?" I said.

Lauren and Ben Jones had been dating for months. They were the happiest couple I knew!

"No way. He's the absolute most perfect guy for me," Lauren said. Her face turned pink, as it always did when she talked about Ben.

"I was hoping to find the perfect guy for our poor, boyfriendless friend here," she teased, turning to Brittany.

Brittany poked Lauren in the side. "Your poor, boyfriendless friend is fine, thank you very much."

She tossed the used tissue into the nearest garbage can and gave her clean shoe a nod of approval.

"The site *is* getting pretty popular," I said,

"thanks to my tech genius—the one, the only, Malcolm Freeman. We uploaded a bunch of new pictures and profiles yesterday."

Brittany glanced down the hall. "Here comes Mary-Kate—finally."

"I know I'm late. Sorry, sorry! But I need your help. Right now!" Mary-Kate rushed over to us. She skidded to a stop and almost dropped her armload of books.

I reached out to steady her stack of books.

"Thanks," Mary-Kate said breathlessly. She threw herself down on the bench.

"If you don't make us guess what you want help with, we'll be able to help you faster," Brittany told her.

Mary-Kate grinned and ran her fingers through her blond hair. "Ms. Barbour assigned me to write the lead story for next week's edition of the school Web page! My first lead!"

"That's so cool!" Lauren exclaimed.

A grin as big as Mary-Kate's broke across her face. When one of her friends is happy, Lauren is happy. Maybe even happier than they are. That's just the way she is.

"Awesome!" I cried.

"You deserve it," Brittany said. "You've been

writing your fingers off lately. What kind of help do you need?"

"I have to come up with a story. The biggest thing ever," Mary-Kate explained.

"What kind of story?" I asked.

"I don't know," Mary-Kate wailed. "That's why I need you guys. So come on—give it up. Thoughts, suggestions, little tiny scraps of ideas. I'll take anything!" She looked at us expectantly.

"I've got one," Brittany said. "How about a story on why parents shouldn't have a baby when they already have a kid in high school? I can give you lots of quotes—because my little brother, Lucas the Mucus, is ruining my life!"

"Lucas the Mucus?" I couldn't help giggling. "That's a new one," I said. "What happened to Caramel-Apple Head and Sweetie Teeny-Toes?"

"That's when I used to think he was cute," Brittany explained.

I knew Brittany still thought her baby brother was cute. Who wouldn't? He had skin just the color of a caramel apple and the longest black eyelashes and the most adorable outie belly button. And his laugh made you laugh, too.

"Do you know how many shirts of mine he's spit up on?" Brittany asked. "I'll tell you: *all* of them. And Mom and Dad don't even bother to ask anymore if I'm free to baby-sit. They just announce they're leaving and the next thing I hear is the door slamming. Any teenager who has a baby in the house can forget about any kind of normal high school life."

"Problem solved?" Lauren asked Mary-Kate.

"Hmmm . . ." Mary-Kate stared off into space. She always does that when she's thinking about a story.

"Thanks for the idea, Britt," she said, "but I'm not seeing it. I'm looking for a story absolutely everybody can relate to."

I leaned my head back on the wall behind me, trying to think. A couple of guys strolled by, and they all took a long look at Mary-Kate. Then they started talking in low whispers. I thought I heard one of them say her name.

I sat up straight. Those guys had better not be gossiping about my sister!

"Did you see that?" I burst out.

"What?" Mary-Kate asked.

"You didn't notice those two guys checking you out?" I asked.

"I was too busy thinking about the story." Mary-Kate smoothed on some lime lip balm. "But why are you so upset? Getting looked at isn't such a bad thing, is it?"

"It's not just the looking. It's the whispering. What is going on at this school all of a sudden?" I cried.

"Do you know what she's talking about?" Mary-Kate asked Lauren and Brittany.

"Everyone seems to be in full-on gossip mode today," Brittany answered.

Lauren nodded. "Bayside High has become the center of whispers and weird looks."

"Really? That's funny. I didn't notice anything like that," Mary-Kate said. "But what else? I need more ideas."

"How about something on the history of the first school prom?" Lauren suggested. "With pictures! I think that could be really cute."

Mary-Kate whipped out a notebook from the rat's nest she calls a backpack. Before she could zip it up again, I saw at least six lip balms, all different flavors; *my* sparkly pink dragonfly barrette; a couple of computer disks; a small stuffed armadillo; and two binders.

"I'm writing that idea down," she told Lauren. "I think it would be a great feature story. But a lead story has to be something everybody's talking about—or will be. Something that affects everybody at school. Like a popular teacher getting fired, or a team winning a championship game."

I let my eyes roam the hallway. There had to be something going on around this school that would make a blockbuster story for Mary-Kate. And I knew she wouldn't give any of us any peace until she found it.

Olivia-and-Jared came around the corner. They're the supercouple of Bayside High School. They're seniors and they've been together since they were freshmen. That's pretty much forever in dating years.

I held up my hands. "Prepare to be dazzled. I have the perfect idea," I announced.

Three pairs of eyes turned to me. I hit them with it.

"'Olivia and Jared: How Does the Perfect Couple Stay That Way?' There's your headline. Think about it. Nobody stays together all four years of high school. They must have a secret."

Lauren gave her version of a touchdown dance without bothering to stand up. "I think we have a winner!" she cried.

"Everyone in school is interested in Jared and Olivia," Brittany agreed, "so you've got guy-and-girl reader appeal. Girls will want to know how they can hook up with someone like Jared long-term, and vice versa."

I checked Mary-Kate's enthusiasm level.

"Hmmm..." she said, tapping her pencil.

"We could team up, Mary-Kate," I said. "I could do a sample compatibility chart for Jared and Olivia on Love Link, and you could interview them for tips on how to stay together."

I invented a special matchmaking system—Ashley Olsen's Theory of Compatibility—one day during math class. It's not so important to have a lot in common with a guy. It's the *ratio* of common interests to common values that matters. (We happened to be studying ratios that day.)

I made up a questionnaire people could fill out about their interests and values. The kids who logged on to Love Link would fill out the questionnaire and post their photos. Then they could scan through the other photos and questionnaires until they found someone they were interested in.

Ashley's Love Link had been up for only a few months, but it was turning into a huge success!

"What do you think, Mary-Kate?" Lauren asked. "Olivia-and-Jared on page one?"

Mary-Kate scribbled away in her notebook.

"High curiosity factor. Wide readership. I'm liking, I'm liking." She hesitated, her pencil hovering over the page. "But I'm liking it for a feature. Not for the top story."

Brittany, Lauren, and I groaned.

"I need a real *news* story," Mary-Kate said. "Everyone *would* want to read about Jared and Olivia, but you've got to admit—they aren't news. Like Ashley said, they've been together for four years."

"So we're looking for news with an emphasis on the *new*. A late-breaking story, a 'we interrupt this program' kind of thing," I said, starting a mental checklist.

Mary-Kate nodded.

"Something juicy," Lauren added.

Mary-Kate nodded again.

"Something that's a Mary-Kate Olsen exclusive," Brittany chimed in.

"Exactly!" Mary-Kate said.

"There's only one problem," Brittany said. "Nothing like that ever happens around here."

"She's right," Lauren agreed. "Nothing exciting ever happens at Bayside High. Except maybe whatever it is that's gotten everybody gossiping!"

"Ashley!" someone screeched.

I whipped my head around.

Michelle Simmons came running up to me. She stopped about an inch away from my face.

"Ashley, how could you do this to me?" she cried. "You have totally ruined my life!"

chapter two

I jumped to my feet. "Calm down, Michelle," I said.

"This isn't about you, Mary-Kate," Michelle shot back. She turned to Ashley. "Why? That's all I want to know." Her hazel eyes glistened. She looked as if she was going to cry.

"What are you talking about?" Ashley asked. She was totally confused.

Michelle swiped at her eyes with the back of her hand. "What I'm talking about is the fact that you gave my picture to the Beauty or Beast Website," she yelled.

"The what?" Ashley said. "I don't even know what that is."

Michelle snorted. "I'll just bet you don't!"

"What's Beauty or Beast?" Lauren asked us.

Brittany shook her head. I shrugged.

Michelle's eyes darted back and forth among the four of us. "Are you kidding? Everyone at school is talking about it!"

"Clearly we're losers who know nothing," Brittany said. "Why don't you give us the scoop?"

"I'm sure Ashley could tell you," Michelle snapped. "Beauty or Beast is a Website where there are pictures of people from school. And whoever goes on the site gets to vote if the people in the pictures are beauties or beasts."

"That explains why I heard a couple of girls call someone a beast in the bathroom a little while ago," Ashley said. Her eyebrows were pulled together.

"I went on the site this morning just for fun," Michelle said, "and whose picture do I find on there? Mine! The very same picture I gave *you* last week for Love Link!"

"Anybody can grab a photo from a Website and copy it onto their own site," I said. "Why do you think this has something to do with Ashley?"

"Yeah," Brittany said. "Haven't you seen those warnings when you're surfing the Net—'Do not remove content from this site without the Webmaster's permission'? That's why those warnings are there. It's really easy to hijack content."

"Brittany and Mary-Kate are right," Ashley said to Michelle. "Somebody must have stolen your picture from my site."

Michelle finally calmed down. "All right. I guess I believe you," she said. "But I'm warning you, Ashley, lots of kids at school think you've been giving pictures to Beauty or Beast." She started to walk off.

A few feet away, she turned around and said over her shoulder, "Some people even think you're running the site yourself!"

Ashley looked stunned.

"Are you okay?" I asked my sister.

"Yeah." Ashley let out a long breath. "We've got to find out everything we can about this Beauty or Beast Website. Right now," she said.

"We've got a little time before first period starts," I said. "Let's hit the library."

We'd taken only three steps before Andrew Leonard planted himself in front of Ashley.

"Hey, what's up Andy Panda?" she said.

"I want you to take me off Love Link," Andrew mumbled, staring down at his sneakers.

"Come on, Andrew. Love Link will come through for you, I promise," Ashley said. She touched his arm. Andrew jerked away and took a step back.

"Just take it off, Ashley. Today," Andrew said. A deep flush crept up the back of his neck. "And take if off your other site, too." He rushed away, head down.

"He wouldn't even look at me." Ashley stared after him. "We played together in *kindergarten* and now he won't even look at me."

"Because of that site," I told her. "You heard what he said. He wants off *both* your sites. He must think the same thing as Michelle—that you have something to do with that other Website."

"We have got to get to the bottom of the Beauty or Beast deal," Brittany said.

"Right!" we all agreed.

Ashley led the way to the library. She walked faster than before.

"Last computer in the first row is free," Lauren called as we headed through the library's automatic doors. I sucked in a lungful of library air as we rushed inside. For some reason the air always feels a little cleaner in there.

Ashley sat down in the chair in front of the computer.

"Go to the BeatFeet search engine first," I

urged. I wanted to squeeze into the chair and take over, but I forced myself to stay still.

Ashley got to the BeatFeet search engine with one click and typed in the words, "Beauty or Beast and Michelle Simmons."

A few seconds later, Ashley gasped. "I think I already see what I'm looking for," she said.

Her voice shook a little. She was more rattled than I thought.

Ashley double-clicked the mouse and a Website came up. The words on top were written in bright pink and electric blue letters.

"Wait," Lauren said, "isn't that Love Link?"

"No, it's not," Ashley said slowly. "The colors are the same ones I use on Love Link. And so is the type."

I took a closer look at the screen. Ashley and Lauren were right. The site looked exactly like Love Link. But at the top of the page were the words "Beauty or Beast—Which One Are You?" Underneath the heading there was a list of names.

Ashley clicked on the first one. A picture loaded.

"That's Rachel Adams!" I exclaimed. "She's my lab partner!"

"Girls," Mr. Sharoff, the librarian, said softly. I jumped. I had no idea he was across the table from us. "Keep it down to a low roar, please."

"Absolutely," Lauren said. Mr. Sharoff nodded and moved away.

"He moves like a fish through water," Brittany whispered. "He could sneak up on anyone. I'm not sure he's human!"

I turned my attention back to the screen. There were radio buttons from one to five under Rachel's picture. To rate Rachel, you clicked on one of the buttons—zero for total beast, five for total beauty. Then a number would flash on the screen—and that was the ranking. Anytime anyone voted, Rachel's ranking would change. Right now it was a 3.2.

"What's that stuff written under her picture?" Brittany asked. She crowded close to me, trying to get nearer to the screen.

"Oh, no!" Ashley said. "It's not just a ranking—people are writing things about each other."

"I notice no one bothered to give their names along with their comments," Lauren said in a disgusted voice.

I read one of the opinions out loud: "'All those hours on the volleyball court have given her a great bod. But I've heard she doesn't shave her pits.'"

"If I wrote something that nasty, I wouldn't

want to put my name on it either," Brittany said. She shook her head.

"Didn't anyone say anything nice?" Lauren asked.

Ashley scrolled down a little. " 'Great gal—on and off the court,'" she read. "'Love her wild sneak collection.'"

"She does have the best sneakers," Brittany said. "Have you seen the lime ones?"

"The jelly ones with the pink laces?" Lauren asked. "So cute!"

Ashley scrolled through the list and clicked on Andrew's name. "I'd better check out Andrew's page," she said. "I've never seen him so upset."

Andrew's picture popped up with a rating of 2.2. Not great.

Ashley read one of the comments: "'Andrew's nice but bo-*ring*. I wouldn't go out with him—unless I was having trouble sleeping at night. Ho-hum.'"

"That's not true!" Lauren cried. "He's quiet, but he's not dull. Whoever wrote that obviously doesn't know Andrew at all."

There were a few other comments, all saying pretty much the same thing.

"Poor Andrew," Ashley said. "Now I can see why he was so hurt."

I glanced at the clock. "Don't you want to check Michelle's page, Ash?" I asked. "We don't have much time left before first period."

"I do, but I don't," Ashley said. "Michelle was so upset. Whatever was written about her must be pretty bad."

But she scrolled down the list until she found Michelle's name. I couldn't believe how long the list was! There must be a page for almost everyone in the school!

"Huh. She's got a 4.7 ranking. Almost a perfect beauty," Brittany said. "There's got to be something ugly in the comments or she wouldn't be running around saying you ruined her life."

"'Michelle is always fun. You should always invite her to a party,'" Ashley read just loudly enough for us to hear. "'Michelle's a cutie. Love the accessories. Love the hair.'"

Brittany shook her head. "Nothing to be upset about in those two."

Ashley scrolled down some more.

"*Uh-oh!*" Lauren exclaimed.

"Lauren, what did you see?" I grabbed her arm. I couldn't wait another second.

"Listen." Lauren leaned over Ashley's shoulder and began to read: "'It was love-love off the tennis court for Michelle and Scott Bennett. At least that's what it looked like since they were k-i-s-s-i-n-g after the match last weekend.'"

"*Yikes!*" I burst out.

Oops. I covered my mouth as I scanned the room for Mr. Sharoff. Whew. There was no sign of him.

"Do you know who Scott Bennett is?" I whispered. "The guy who Michelle is supposed to have been kissing?"

"He's in my history class," Brittany said. "Smart, quiet, always wears T-shirts with political slogans."

"You want another factoid about him?" I said. "Scott Bennett is Zoe Farrell's boyfriend. And Zoe Farrell is Michelle Simmons's doubles tennis partner."

Lauren's mouth dropped open. "So Michelle is sneaking around with her tennis partner's guy? That's so low," she said.

"Just because somebody posted it on a Website doesn't mean it's true," Ashley reminded her.

"Yeah. Would Michelle have been so upset if it were true? Wouldn't she be walking around school hiding her head, totally ashamed of herself?" Brittany asked.

Lauren twisted a piece of her long brown ponytail around two fingers. "I don't know. Maybe she was that upset because the truth was out."

I nudged Ashley out of her chair. I *had* to see more of the site. Prickles ran all the way down my spine. I always get prickles when I think I'm on to a fantastic story. And I had the feeling this Beauty or Beast site was going to be the perfect lead story for next week's edition of the school Web page!

"I really don't think Michelle is the kind of person who would go after another girl's boyfriend," I heard Ashley say. Then I tuned out the rest of the conversation as I scrolled through the site as fast as I could.

Paula Cooper was ranked exactly halfway between beauty and beast. Someone wanted to walk barefoot in her beautiful hair. Someone else would have ranked her a five if it weren't for her voice—much too squeaky.

John Lee was ranked at 1.1. Ouch! Almost one hundred percent beast. I would never rank him that way. Not that I'd actually want to rank anyone at all.

I scanned the comments. One near the top said that there was absolute confirmation that John had the worst case of acne ever. Almost every post after that mentioned acne. *So that one comment must have completely ruined his ranking*, I thought.

I scrolled through some more entries, then smiled. Now, this was a guy whose info I was totally curious about. He was ranked a five. A one hundred percent beauty. I wasn't surprised. Aaron, my sister's boyfriend, is a hottie—tall, athletic, with longish wavy hair.

I read the first comment to myself. *Aaron's a guy you can talk to about anything*. Yeah, that fit. He really listened. And he really cared. What more could you ask for?

"Ashley, you should read—"

Wait. No. I definitely didn't want Ashley to read the second comment.

"Hey, is that Aaron's picture?" Ashley asked.

I clicked on the next name. Why had I opened my big mouth so fast?

"No. Unh-unh. Nope," I said, my words bumping into one another.

"But you just flipped to Rachel Moore's picture. And the site is organized alphabetically," Ashley said.

Why does she have to be so logical? Why? Why? Why? I asked myself. If she were more like me, she wouldn't have picked up on the alphabetizing so fast. I hadn't noticed.

Brittany reached around me and clicked on the BACK key. Ashley and Lauren leaned over my shoulders.

Ashley gasped. "Aaron is dating someone else?"

chapter three

"It's not true," Lauren said, wrapping her arm around me. "You know that. Anyone who knows Aaron even a little knows that."

I closed my eyes for a second. Then I opened them and forced myself to read the message out loud: "'Ashley Olsen better watch out. Her guy is crushing on someone new. Well, she shouldn't feel too bad. It's hard to hang on to one of the school's fives.'"

"Someone was in a nasty mood the day they wrote that," Brittany said. "Let it roll right off you. Like water off a duck's back."

"Quack," Lauren whispered helpfully.

I gave my friends a quick smile, then turned my attention back to the computer screen. I wanted to read everything that was written about Aaron.

"Let's get out of here. The bell is going to ring any second," Mary-Kate urged.

"One more sec." I looked at the next post. This was it. This was what Mary-Kate was trying to protect me from.

"'I've seen Aaron out with another girl three times,'" I read out loud. "'Any bets on how many days until he dumps Ashley? I say a week tops.'"

Brittany reached out and punched the power button on the computer. The screen went black.

"We aren't reading any more of these lies!" she said. "Just because somebody has nothing better to do with their time than write a bunch of—"

I heard loud footsteps behind me. I turned and saw Mr. Sharoff.

"How many warnings have I given you girls?" he demanded. This time he didn't bother to keep his voice low.

"Um, one?" Mary-Kate said.

"Two," I said. Which maybe wasn't the smartest thing to say. But two was the right answer.

"That's right. Which is two more than I should have given you," Mr. Sharoff snapped. "Now you've got three strikes and you're out of the game." He jerked his thumb toward the door.

My cheeks began to burn. I glanced at Lauren and saw that her face was already so red you couldn't see her freckles. I'd never been kicked out of the library before. I'd never been kicked out of *anywhere*. None of us had.

But all we could do was gather up our stuff and take the walk of shame with everyone watching us—watching and whispering. I was starting to hate the sound of whispering.

Lauren led me out of the library and over to the closest drinking fountain.

"Have a drink," she instructed. "You'll feel better."

I obeyed. And the cool water did help. It was as if it rinsed my brain so I could think clearly again.

"Are you all right?" Mary-Kate asked.

"Do you want to sit down? There's an empty bench right over there," Brittany said.

"Maybe you should have some more water," Lauren said.

I looked from worried face to worried face and smiled.

"You know what? I'm fine," I announced. "I was shocked for a minute. But I really am fine now."

"You are?" Lauren blurted out. "Why?"

Brittany tugged Lauren's ponytail. "What kind of question is that?" she asked.

I laughed. "It's okay, Lauren," I said. "I was thinking about what you said in the library. It's totally true. Anybody who knows Aaron knows the junk about him on the Website isn't true. And I know Aaron better than anybody, so—"

"So you're absolutely positive it isn't true," Mary-Kate finished for me.

"I'm sure nothing on Beauty or Beast is true," Brittany added.

"It's like the whole thing was created just to make people feel bad," I said. "Oh—that explains Alicia Gorman!"

"What about her?" Lauren asked.

"I ran into her in the bathroom this morning. She was acting really strange," I said. "She was worried she had a nose only a pug dog could love."

Suddenly I felt a burst of hot anger rise inside me. "I bet that pug-dog line is a direct quote from Alicia's Beauty or Beast page!"

"Well, at least we know what all the gossiping is about," Brittany said. "Everyone is whispering about what they read on the site."

"Checking people out and wondering if what they read is true," Lauren added.

"We've got to stop it," I said. "Not just because some kids think I have something to do with the site, but because it's a horrible site whose only purpose is to make people feel bad about themselves!"

"You're right, Ashley," Mary-Kate said. "This is going to be my lead story. I'm going to do an article about Beauty or Beast. I'm going to expose it for what it is—all gossip and lies."

"Great idea," Brittany said. "That's exactly what news stories should do."

"And *I'm* going to find out exactly who is behind the site," I said. "Whoever it is who stole all the pictures from my Love Link site!"

"Right," Lauren said. "That should be part of the story too. Nobody should be able to get away with hurting so many people."

"By the time we're through, every single person at this school is going to know that the Beauty or Beast site is full of gossip and lies," I said.

"Absolutely." Lauren gave my arm an encouraging squeeze. "Now I can see why Michelle was so upset. Can you imagine what that nasty little comment about her and Zoe's boyfriend could do? It could split up Zoe and Scott."

"It could split up Michelle and Zoe, too,"

Brittany said. "Would you want to be tennis partners with a girl you thought was trying to steal your boyfriend?"

"At least Michelle finally believed you didn't have anything to do with her photo showing up on the site," Mary-Kate said.

"That's one person out of the whole school," I reminded her. "We have to find out who the Beauty or Beast Webmaster is. And fast."

chapter four

"How's it going out there, Mary-Kate?" Ms. Barbour called from her office.

"Great!" It was Friday afternoon. As soon as the last bell rang, I rushed directly to my desk in the school Website room. For the last hour I'd been pounding away on my story nonstop.

Actually, it was more of an editorial now. In a real news story, a reporter has to give just the facts and keep her feelings out of it. But I felt so strongly about the Beauty or Beast Website, I couldn't keep my opinion to myself. So I talked Ms. Barbour into letting me put an editorial in the lead spot. I thought this issue deserved it.

I scrolled back to the top to read over the beginning of my piece:

A terrible disease has infected Bayside High—and it's spreading fast. Gossip. It's vicious. It's mean. And it hurts everyone it touches.

You've seen people whispering. You've heard the rumors. You know where it all started—the Beauty or Beast Website.

This Website claims to tell us who is beautiful and who is not. Who is cheating with whom. Who is lying to whom. But the site was set up anonymously, and the comments are all anonymous as well. Most of the rumors on the site are outright lies. But everyone reads them anyway. And repeats them—until the damage is done.

I know the people at this school. I know you're not mean. I know you don't want to hurt each other. But the Beast is taking on a life of its own. It feeds off everyone who visits the site, everyone who ranks one of their fellow students or writes a comment about them. It is out of control.

We can't allow this to go on. We have to join together and stop the Beast. I promise to investigate and find out who started the Website. In the meantime, don't log on to Beauty or Beast. Resist the temptation to rate people and write comments. We've got to stop this gossip virus before it's too late.

I hit the SAVE button and leaned back in my desk chair with a sigh of satisfaction.

"That's the sound of someone who has just completed a hard task," Ms. Barbour said. "Would you like a mint brownie to revive yourself?" She stepped out of her office holding a plate.

"Wow, thanks, Ms. Barbour!" I said. "I'm starving!"

I hurried over to her and took a brownie. Brownies with peppermint are were Ms. Barbour's specialty. Actually, brownies were the only thing she could cook, she once told us.

"Mind if I take a look at your story?" Ms. Barbour asked.

"Sure," I mumbled through the delicious mix of sweet and tart. "It's still up on my computer."

I watched her out of the corner of my eye as she walked over to my computer and started to read.

I took another bite of brownie and tried not to look at Ms. Barbour. I always get nervous when someone is reading my work—especially Ms. Barbour. But my eyes kept sliding over there. So I focused on her clothes instead of the expression on her face.

Ms. Barbour used to work at *Fashion Daily*

magazine in New York. She still knows the very latest fashions—and wears them.

Today she had on a light blue skirt with a huge green bird on it. On top she wore a plain white shirt with a V-neck. She didn't have on any jewelry at all. Probably because the bird was enough for anybody to look at!

"Wonderful stuff, Mary-Kate," Ms. Barbour finally said, putting me out of my misery. "Strong and sharp as usual. Persuasive too."

"Thanks!" I didn't know what else to say. I always wanted Ms. Barbour to love what I wrote. But when she gave me a compliment, I got a little tongue-tied.

"Do you think you could give me a peek at the site?" Ms. Barbour asked. "I'm intrigued."

"Of course. I can't wait to hear what you think of it," I said. I brought up the Beauty or Beast site on my computer screen.

"Click on a name to look at that person's page," I told Ms. Barbour.

Ms. Barbour scanned the list and clicked on the very last name, Jason Zigler. Jason was rated an even 3.0, perfectly in the middle.

I think Jason's hot, wrote one person who gave him a 4.0. *I like the brainy type*.

Are you crazy? wrote another person. *He picks his nose. I saw him! He's a 2.0, tops.*

After a few minutes Ms. Barbour looked up at me. "This is . . ." She shook her head as if she couldn't come up with the right words to describe it. And Ms. Barbour is an English teacher and adviser for the school Website. She can *always* come up with the right words.

"I can see why you are so upset." Ms. Barbour frowned at the screen. "Creating this Website didn't take much thought or effort. But it's going to hurt a lot of people."

"And it's hurt Ashley's reputation," I said. "I can't believe anybody would think she would have anything to do with that site."

Ms. Barbour closed the Web page. "I'm proud of you for taking on this subject, Mary-Kate. It's timely. And more than that, your article can have an effect on people's lives. That's an honor and a responsibility."

"Wow. Thanks, Ms. Barbour." Again, it was all that I could think of to say.

"If you weren't writing the story, I'd bring it to the principal's attention myself," Ms. Barbour said. "But this is exactly the kind of thing our school Website should bring to light."

"I think so too, Ms. Barbour," I said. "I want to convince everyone to boycott the site."

"I know you can do it, Mary-Kate." Ms. Barbour smiled. "As much as I hate to admit it, I can understand why so many people are intrigued by the site. It must be difficult to resist the temptation to find out what others are saying about you."

I was totally surprised to hear her say that. "Ummm . . . I guess."

"I have to run down to the main office. You stay and work as long as you need to. I'll be back to lock up." With that, Ms. Barbour breezed out the door.

I pulled my article back up on the screen and started typing. But I couldn't get the words to flow like they had earlier. Ms. Barbour's words kept ringing through my head. *Find out what others are saying about you. Find out what others are saying about you.* That's when I realized that I hadn't looked at *my* page yet.

Don't do it, I told myself. *It doesn't matter what anyone thinks of you.*

But how could I write an article telling everyone to boycott the site if I didn't study it closely? And wasn't studying the site part of my research? So wasn't it my responsibility to go on the site as much as possible?

Except I'd really done all the research on the site I needed.

Still, a little more couldn't hurt. You can't do too much research, right?

My fingers started to itch. I'd take one quick look at my ranking and comments, then I'd log off and go home. And I'd never visit the site again.

I had the Beauty or Beast site open in a flash. I scrolled down to the *O*'s and clicked on my name. It took only a few seconds to load, but the seconds felt like hours.

I bit my lip as I looked for my ranking. It was 4.8! I was a beauty. Almost a total beauty! Whew! That was a relief. I knew I shouldn't care how I was rated, but still . . . I'm only human.

I glanced quickly down the screen. There was a bunch of comments. Should I read them? They weren't that important to me or anything. But I couldn't help myself. I just let myself take in a word here and there—"fun," "shiny lips," "easy to talk to," "want on my team," "smells good," "Oh, Saaandy!"

That last one made me smile from ear to ear. Someone clearly liked my performance in *Grease*! I scrolled down. But there were no more comments.

And that was fine. I didn't want people talking

about me on a site like Beauty or Beast anyway.

I logged off, stood up, and gathered my stuff together. As I started toward the door, I realized I was humming "Summer Loving." That was one of my big numbers in *Grease*. I wondered who had written that Sandy comment.

I pulled the door open and stepped into the hallway.

My disk! I thought. I realized I'd forgotten to bring the disk my article was on. I wanted to do some editing on it over the weekend. It was still pretty rough in places.

I hesitated, my hand on the doorknob. Then I started to hum another song from *Grease*. Well, the Beauty or Beast editorial could wait until Monday. I started down the hall, still humming. I didn't care what anybody thought of me. Not at all. But I was glad they didn't hate me. I couldn't help it.

"Okay, Ashley, what you do next is open your mouth, insert the tip of the pizza, and chew," Aaron teased. He gave my hand a gentle nudge.

How long had I been holding the slice of black olive pizza an inch in front of my mouth? I quickly took a bite, and gave Aaron a close-lipped smile while I chewed.

"What were you thinking about?" he asked. "You were really out of it for a minute there."

It was Friday night—date night. We were at Lucio's Pizzeria, one of those places with candles on each table in wine-bottle holders. The bottles have colored wax dripped over them. Lucio's was packed with couples out on dates and kids out with their friends.

"I was thinking about Beauty or Beast," I admitted.

"Can't you take a break from worrying about it?" Aaron asked. He gave the pizza tin a flick and it spun in wobbly circles. For a couple of hours at least? Your brain needs to relax."

I took a deep breath and smiled. "You're right. My brain and the rest of me need a break."

I took a sip of my soda. "But it was just so horrible seeing people look at me like they . . . like they hated me!"

And it was even more horrible to read that Aaron was seeing someone else, I thought. But I was determined not to mention it. I wouldn't let it get to me.

"No one is looking at you right now—except me. And I don't hate you," Aaron said. He leaned in and gave me a quick peck on the lips.

"You're right." I took another bite of pizza. And I almost choked. Because Aaron was wrong. Three people were glaring at me from the back booth—Jennifer O'Leary, Lissa Burns, and Cindy Cole.

All three girls looked like they wished I'd keep on choking.

I managed to swallow my bite of pizza.

"Do you need some water?" Aaron asked.

I nodded, and he handed me a glass. I drank it down. Jennifer, Lissa, and Cindy watched me without blinking.

I set down the glass. "I just need to run to the ladies' room for a sec," I told Aaron.

I slid out of the red leather booth and rushed to the bathroom.

Okay, Ashley, take a second and get ahold of yourself, I thought. *So you got some nasty looks. So what?*

I headed to the mirror and started to repair the makeup damage the choking and water chugging had done.

The bathroom door swung open. I jerked my head toward the sound—and accidentally drew a line of baby-kiss-pink lip liner from the corner of my mouth halfway across my cheek.

Lissa, Cindy, and Jennifer stepped into the bathroom.

"Hey, Ashley," Jennifer said. She didn't *sound* mad.

"Hi, guys," I answered. I grabbed a tissue out of my purse. Carefully, I began wiping away the lip-liner smear.

"We're just having a girls' night out," Cindy told me.

"Fun." The lip liner wasn't completely wiping away. I decided to try a little concealer on top.

"Not really," Lissa said. "Do you know why it's a girls' night out? Because all of a sudden we have no boyfriends. Thanks to you and that Website."

"Yeah, suddenly Kyle has decided my arms are—to quote from Beauty or Beast—'floppy,'" Cindy announced. "And he can't stop thinking about it. So he wants to just be friends."

"That's pretty shallow—" I started to say.

"Breen thinks I've been going out with my old boyfriend," Lissa interrupted. "So he wants nothing to do with me. Even though I've told him it's not true a million times."

"And Ryan now thinks that so many girls would love the chance to go out with him that he wants us both to be able to date other people,"

Jennifer said. "We just wanted you to know what your site did to our lives."

She turned around. Lissa and Cindy immediately headed for the door after her.

"It's not my site, you guys!" I called after them. "I'm trying to figure out who started it. Didn't you see all the rumors about Aaron and another girl? Why would I want something like that on my own Website?"

Cindy turned back. "Looks like you've created a monster," she sneered.

"That's a lie. Just like it's a lie that Lissa's going out with an old boyfriend," I said.

Cindy, Jennifer, and Lissa left without saying another word. They wanted to talk. But they didn't want to listen.

Then I left, too, and headed back to our table.

Aaron took one look at my face and said, "You're still thinking about it, I can tell."

I sighed and nodded.

"Look—we're not going to have any fun as long as you're worrying about Beauty or Beast," he said. "So why don't we try to figure out who could have started the site?"

"Thanks, Aaron. You're the best." I was so happy he understood. "I'll feel a lot better once

44

everyone knows for sure that I don't have anything to do with Beauty or Beast."

Aaron gave the pizza pan another spin. "We need to think like FBI profilers. What kind of person creates a site like Beauty or Beast?"

"Someone who doesn't like me?" I guessed.

"No. I don't think the Webmaster thought everyone would blame you," Aaron said. "I think he or she just snatched pictures from your site because it was easy."

"Hmmm. I read an article in *GirlTime* that said a lot of times people who make fun of other people turn out to be insecure themselves," I said.

I took another bite of my pizza slice and gave the crust to Aaron. He loves to eat the crusts.

"That's the kind of thing we need for our criminal profile." His blue eyes burned with excitement. "Item one—insecurity. What else?"

"Well, definitely someone with access to a computer and better-than-average computer skills." I pulled my glitter notebook out of my purse.

"Good, good." Aaron ate his crust in two bites. "But that one doesn't eliminate a whole lot of people at our school."

"True. Everybody knows something about

computers at Bayside. And there are tons of computers around," I agreed.

Aaron frowned, thinking hard. "I bet that whoever runs the site doesn't have a boyfriend or a girlfriend. Just a gut feeling."

"I agree." I wrote that down too. "So we've got an insecure guy or girl without a romantic attachment who can use a computer."

It was a start. But it didn't give me much to go on.

chapter five

Saturday evening I was off to Click Café to meet Malcolm. He helped me build Love Link. He was the perfect person to help me figure out who was behind Beauty or Beast.

The drive to Click was too short. I knew there might be kids from school in the coffeehouse, and I was so not ready for more attitude. But I went inside. What choice did I have?

I looked around. There were only two people from Bayside in Click. Well, three, counting Malcolm. Olivia-and-Jared sat on a deep cushy couch all the way in the back. I didn't have to worry about them. They never noticed anyone but each other.

"Are you ready to save my life?" I called as I walked over to Malcolm. He was fooling around with the computer on the table in front of him. There are computers all over Click.

Malcolm slapped the spot on the couch next to him. "I already did, of course."

"Really?" My eyes widened.

"Well, I knew you didn't want Love Link to look anything like Beauty or Beast," Malcolm explained. "So I redesigned Love Link by changing the colors. See?"

"That's great, Malcolm. Thanks so much. But what I really need is—"

"Oh, and I made a new banner, too," Malcolm said. "It says that Love Link has no connection to Beauty or Beast."

"Wow. You really thought of everything." I gave him a quick hug. "But there's something else I need your help with. Something a lot bigger."

Malcolm raised one eyebrow. "How much bigger?" he asked warily.

"I have to find out who created the Beauty or Beast site. Is it possible to do that on line?" I asked. "Please say it is."

"That depends," Malcolm said. "It's going to cost you, you know."

"How much?" I asked.

"I'll have to think about it." He cracked his

knuckles once, then twice. "But be prepared to spend most of next week baking cookies, brownies, cupcakes . . ." He hunched over the keyboard and started clicking away. "And any kind of new snack treats you might want to invent."

"You got it," I promised.

I sat back and watched Malcolm work his magic. I love the sound of the clicking and clacking of a computer keyboard. To me, it's the sound of things being accomplished. And I couldn't wait to find out who was behind Beauty or Beast!

"Okay, the site is hosted by the school server," Malcolm said. "That means it's definitely a Bayside kid. Or a teacher, but that's, like, no way."

"I knew it!" I said.

I leaned over Malcolm's shoulder. We were closing in on our prey. He was right. It couldn't be a teacher. Why would a teacher do something like this? But a Bayside student? Definitely.

Malcolm began clicking the keys again. I tapped my toes. I couldn't sit still.

Cruughk. A horrible grinding noise filled the café.

Malcolm shoved himself to his feet. "The new girl is totally wrecking the espresso machine."

"But you're not working today," I protested.

"I know, but—"

Cruughk.

"She'll ruin it," Malcolm said. "Not that I care. But some people in this joint, you don't give them their espresso, they bite your head off. And I'd like to keep my head on if I can. Be right back." He slouched away.

"I don't ever want to see you again!" a girl yelled.

"I don't care!" a guy shouted back. "I hate you!"

I turned toward the voices, trying to see what was going on without looking like I was snooping.

My jaw dropped when I saw who it was. Jared-and-Olivia! They were sitting on one of the green sofas in the back. As I watched, Olivia jerked on her maroon suede jacket and got up.

"There is no possible way you *could* hate me more than I hate you. I can't believe I wasted four years of my life with you!" Olivia cried.

I felt as if I'd stumbled into some alternate universe or a science-fiction movie. This had to be everything-backward land. Jared and Olivia never had fights. Never.

But they were fighting today. Olivia stormed past me. Her cheeks were wet with tears.

I took a peek back at Jared. He sat slumped on the couch, his head resting against the back wall.

I got up and headed toward him. I don't even really know Jared. But he looked so miserable, I had to at least try to cheer him up.

"Um, hey," I said when I reached him.

"Did I actually say I hated her?" he asked without lifting his head.

"I didn't really hear," I said. "Um, so, are you okay?"

"No," Jared said. "Olivia went on that moronic site—Beauty or Beast—and some clown wrote that I was after Jenny, who is Olivia's best friend."

"Yikes!" I said.

"Yikes, yeah," he repeated. "What gets me is she believed it right off. After all this time."

"A lot of people have been having problems because of that site," I told him. "And everything on there is lies. My sister is writing an article on it for the school Website. Maybe that will help."

Jared lifted his head and looked at me for the first time. "It might be too late. She *believed* it."

He stood up, grabbed his backpack, and dragged himself out of the café.

I returned to my seat. Malcolm was still behind the counter. He patted the gold eagle on top of the espresso machine as he talked to the new counter girl.

Poor Jared, I thought. *And poor Olivia.* I was glad I didn't believe what I read about Aaron on Beauty or Beast.

Suddenly I wondered if there were any new posts on Aaron's page. I couldn't stop the thought from popping into my head.

I shot another glance at Malcolm. It looked as if he'd be a while, so I slid in front of the computer and pulled up the Beauty or Beast Website. A moment later my boyfriend's face was smiling at me.

I smiled back. I couldn't not smile when I looked at Aaron. I quickly scrolled down the comments.

Aaron's really smart. He reminds me of Joel on Spencer Academy.

I agreed with that one. That's why Joel was my favorite character on that show.

Aaron is the hottest boy in school. How can I get him to notice me?

Get your own boyfriend! I thought.

"Ashley, you want something?" Malcolm called. "I'll get slave girl here to bring it over." He gestured toward the girl behind the counter, who frowned.

"I'll have a decaf coffee, please," I answered.

I scrolled down to the next comment. My stomach twisted into a ball as I read it.

Aaron sighting. On Saturday afternoon I saw Aaron at the Santa Monica Pier, hand in hand with a blonde who wasn't *Ashley. Does he have one girlfriend in Santa Monica and one in Malibu?*

I took a deep breath. *It's the Beauty or Beast site*, I reminded myself. *Everything on it is lies.*

But did it really makes sense that *nobody* posted the truth? Not one person?

"Here you go." Malcolm handed me my coffee in a soup-bowl-size cup.

"Anything new?" he asked, nodding at the Beauty or Beast site still up on the screen. "Is Aaron secretly married to a space girl from Venus?"

"Not quite that bad," I said. "But almost." I closed Aaron's page and slid over so Malcolm could get behind the computer again.

Malcolm's fingers flew over the keyboard. "And we now know the person who created the site. Screen name anyway. It's . . . hold on . . . got it! Someone named TurtleShell."

I gave a little squeal of joy. I couldn't help myself.

"What kind of cheeseball picks a screen name like that? Inquiring minds want to know." Malcolm hunched even closer to the keyboard. I hunched right along with him.

Click, clack, click, click.

Malcolm let out a grunt. "Nope. Sorry. I was trying to access the list that matches student names with their screen names. But it's classified."

"You still found out a lot," I said, patting him on the shoulder. "Now all I have to do is find out who TurtleShell is and I can clear my name!"

chapter six

First thing Sunday morning my eyes flew open. Beauty or Beast was on my mind.

It was driving me crazy. I promised Ashley I'd help her find out who was behind it. Actually, I promised the whole school.

But after spending all day Saturday investigating, I'd gotten nowhere. I talked to all my friends. I asked them if anyone they knew was acting suspiciously. Malcolm said he thought the whole school was in some kind of pro-Westwood conspiracy. Westwood High is Bayside's biggest rival. Malcolm was not being helpful.

I went through the school directory to see if anyone's name triggered anything. I even called Ms. Drews, the computer teacher, to see if she knew anything.

There was nothing to do but check the Website for clues. Maybe the Webmaster had written something on the site. Or maybe I could find some kind of pattern. . . .

While I was there, I thought I might as well check my own page. Not that I cared or anything. But what if the Webmaster knew I was looking for him or her? What if he or she had left a clue for me on my page?

I'd better check, I thought.

I logged on to the Beauty or Beast site and clicked on my name.

"That's strange," I muttered. My ranking had dropped from 4.8 to 4.6. Why? How had this happened? I couldn't have suddenly just become more beastly. Could I?

I stared at the computer screen. There must be some explanation. Were there any new comments?

I scrolled down past the comments I'd already read. There were three new ones.

I read the first one.

Mary-Kate is a nice girl and everything. I love her hair, the way it's so wavy. But, I got to say, her look is a little . . . zzzz.

I swallowed hard. *That's just one person's opinion,* I told myself. *Everybody has different tastes.* I forced myself to read the next comment.

I like everything about Mary-Kate.

I smiled. That was nice. I continued reading.

But why is she such a Goody Two shoes?

My mouth fell open. I was *not* a Goody Two shoes. Just last week I'd gotten kicked out of the library!

There was one more new comment. I summoned my strength and plowed through it.

You'd think a popular girl like Mary-Kate wouldn't be so desperate—but I heard she's been chasing Craig Withers! She calls him at home and everything!

Who? I thought. I didn't even know who that was.

Oh, yes I did. Craig Withers.

An extremely geeky guy. Thick glasses. Into building model engines. Terrified of girls. Once during an assembly I asked him for the time and he almost had a nervous breakdown.

I actually heard Mary-Kate call Craig a "super-stud." Can you believe it? Maybe she needs glasses!

She should borrow Craig's. They're so thick you can see molecules with them.

This is great, just great, I thought. Now people were out-and-out lying about me!

I paced around my room. What should I do? Nobody would believe the Craig Withers rumor, right? I barely knew the guy. And who cared what people thought anyway? Wasn't that the whole point of my article?

My pacing took me past the full-length mirror on the back of my door. I paused to take a look. Cargo pants. My favorite little light blue tank. Chunky sandals. Two silver toe rings. Was this boring? I thought I looked cute.

I sat back down at my desk. I closed down Beauty or Beast and tried to forget about it.

"Now, where's my disk for English?" I muttered as I fished through my backpack. It didn't take too long to find it. I use green disks for all my writing. Green seems creative to me, I guess because it reminds me of growing things.

I reached out to stick the disk in the drive. My hand froze. I couldn't stop looking at the picture of me, Ashley, Brittany, and Lauren I had on my bulletin board.

It was a picture of the four of us at the beach last summer. Brittany and I were both wearing jean jackets. Lauren and I both had on short skirts with little flowers on them. And Ashley and I wore plain white T-shirts.

But with her jean jacket, Brittany had on a pair of orange-and-yellow-striped bell bottoms. With her flowered skirt, Lauren wore a T-shirt with a grinning gorilla. And Ashley had pulled a vintage brocade vest over her T-shirt.

My clothes were just a combination of what the other three wore. Did that make me dull?

Stop thinking about it, I told myself. *You look like most of the girls at school, and they all look good.*

I knew the rumor about me and Craig Withers wasn't true. So why did I believe the person who criticized my look? It was ridiculous!

I worked on my English paper for an hour or so. Then I turned off my computer and reached for my jacket. I had plans to meet Brittany at the mall. She was dying to get out of the house, which she was now calling "Babyland."

Without really thinking about it, I stopped in front of the mirror for a routine inspection.

Hmm . . . I thought. *Something just doesn't seem right about what I'm wearing today. I think I'll change.*

I took off my cargo pants and changed into jeans. Then I reached for the red gingham top I'd been wearing a lot lately. I paused. No, not the red gingham top. I wanted something different.

I rummaged through all my old clothes and found a shirt I used to love back when I was in second grade. It had the Gooseberry cereal goose on it. And now it fit like a belly shirt. So I put it on and added a candy necklace that had been lying around since Halloween, and my lavender sneakers.

I looked at my reflection in the mirror. There. That was better.

I went downstairs to the kitchen, grabbed a cereal bar, and then headed out the door.

I climbed into the Mustang convertible that Ashley and I share and drove off. Brittany was waiting in the driveway when I reached her house.

"Didn't want to risk getting asked to baby-sit," she told me as she jumped in. She glanced at me and added, "Nice T-shirt. New?"

I shook my head. "I've had it since second grade."

"Cool," Brittany said. "It's not your usual look, but I like it. It's funky."

I grinned. Funky was definitely not dull.

We parked at the mall and headed to Pancake Palace for a late breakfast. Pancake Palace was a popular Sunday-morning hangout for Bayside kids.

"Have you checked out Beauty or Beast lately?" I asked Brittany after we'd ordered.

"No," she said. "And I'm not going to. That Website is totally worthless."

"I know," I agreed. "But I'm trying to help Ashley figure out who set it up. So I looked at my page today, hoping to find a clue."

"Did you find one?" Brittany asked.

"No," I admitted. "Unless you think this is a clue—somebody wrote that I was hot for Craig Withers."

Brittany laughed. "Craig Withers? You mean that guy who tapes pictures of combustion engines to the inside of his locker?"

I nodded. "You don't think he could have started that rumor, do you?" I asked. "Or be involved in the Website?"

"Craig? No way," Brittany said. "He's too shy. His hand would shake just typing a girl's name."

"But who would write something like that? It's obviously a lie."

Brittany shrugged. "Maybe it's the same person who's writing about Ashley and Aaron. I think somebody's jealous of both of you."

"Maybe," I said. "You don't think anybody will believe it, do you?" I asked. "About me chasing after Craig?"

Brittany laughed again. "No, I don't think so.

That's just a little too unbelievable," she said.

Caroline Farber saw us and stopped by our table. "Hey, girls," she said. "Great T-shirt, Mary-Kate."

"Thanks," I said, pleased. Caroline Farber was heavily into fashion.

"I bet Craig Withers will love it when he sees it," she teased.

I rolled my eyes. "You can't believe anything you read on Beauty or Beast."

Caroline smiled. "I don't know," she joked. "I mean, it's so weird that you've got to ask yourself, who would make up something like that?"

"Stop teasing, Caroline," Brittany said. "That Website is causing a lot of trouble."

"I know. I'm sorry," Caroline said. "Don't worry, Mary-Kate. If anyone brings it up, I'll set them straight."

"Thanks, Caroline," I said.

Brittany and I finished our pancakes, paid our check, and headed for an early movie.

"I can't believe I'm hungry again already," Brittany complained when we left the theater. "Pancakes never stick with me. Why is that, Mary-Kate?"

"It's lunchtime anyway," I said. "Let's shop a little and then grab something."

We stopped at Zipper, the coolest boutique in the mall. Brittany pulled a denim skirt off the rack and held it out.

"This looks like something you'd wear," she said. "It would look great on you."

I studied the skirt. It was basic, no-frills, knee-length denim.

"You think so?" I said. "You don't find it a little . . . blah?"

Brittany looked at the skirt. "Not really," she said. "It depends what you wear with it."

"What about this?" I asked, yanking a shiny dress made of clanking metal squares off the rack.

Brittany stared at it. "That? That's too wild for you."

"Why?" I asked, holding the dress up against my body. It was short but looked like it would fit. "You think I can't pull it off?"

"It's not that," Brittany said. "I just think you'd get a lot more wear out of a denim skirt than a silver disco dress. I mean, when's the last time you went to a disco?"

I put the dress back on the rack. "Let's go get some lunch," I said.

We went to Gourmet Garden because Brittany has a thing for their veggie sandwich.

"Oh, no," Brittany said as we approached the entrance. "Look who's standing right outside the door."

A skinny guy with curly brown hair and thick glasses stared at us from in front of the sandwich shop. His plaid pants were too tight over his rubbery legs, and his big puppy-dog feet flopped around in a pair of crepe-soled shoes. He looked about twelve even though he was fifteen. (He skipped third grade.) He was chewing on a pen, with four more crammed into his shirt pocket in case he ran out. It was Craig Withers.

"What are we going to do?" I whispered. "What if he thinks I'm in love with him?"

"He'll never get up the nerve to say anything," Brittany said. "Just keep walking."

"Do you have to have a veggie sandwich?" I asked her. "Wouldn't you like a burger instead?"

"No," she said. "I can't believe you're afraid of Craig Withers."

She marched me up to the Gourmet Garden entrance. I kept waiting for Craig to flinch and run away. But he didn't. Beauty or Beast had made him bold.

"Hi, Mary-Kate," he said. "Um, I need to talk to you."

Oh, no. I glanced at Brittany. She grinned and said, "I'll leave you two alone. Meet me inside."

Thanks a lot, I thought as she disappeared into the sandwich shop. "What is it, Craig?" I asked.

Please don't ask me out. Please don't ask me out, I silently begged. I didn't want to hurt Craig's feelings. But I didn't need Ashley's Theory of Compatibility to know that he and I were not exactly Romeo and Juliet material.

He cleared his throat. "Mary-Kate, I've heard certain rumors and . . ." A look of panic flashed through his eyes and for a second I thought he was going to run away. But he didn't.

". . . well, I know how you feel about me," he said.

My heart sank. "Craig—" I began.

The panicked look crossed his face again and his hands began to tremble.

"Please—don't make this any harder than it already is," he said, staring at his feet. "I just have to tell you that my mother won't let me go out with girls yet. She says I'm too young. But I don't want to upset you, so . . ."

He looked up at me now and took a deep breath. Whatever he wanted to say next was going to take some courage.

"We could go out behind her back," he finished. "She doesn't have to know. There's a mechanical physics convention this weekend. She could drop me off, and we could meet there. In secret."

I opened my mouth. Nothing came out. What could I say?

He was getting braver. "I was going to tell you we couldn't go out because of my mother, but now that I'm here, standing in front of you and actually talking to you, who cares what Mother wants?" He giggled. He was getting giddy. "I don't have to listen to her. I'm fifteen years old!"

This was getting out of hand. I had to put a stop to it before he turned from a shy little nerd to a hormone-crazed rebel.

"Craig, I appreciate that you don't want to hurt me," I said. "But I think we'd better listen to your mother. She knows best, and I don't want to get you in trouble with her."

He looked disappointed and relieved at the same time, if that's possible.

"Yeah, you're right," he said, retreating back

into his shell. "Maybe next year, when I have my license."

"Maybe next year," I said. "I'll just have to hope and pray that you don't fall for someone else by then."

"Yeah," he said. "Well, okay. I'd better run. Bye!"

He turned and ran away without looking back. His big feet made a *flap-flap* sound.

Whew. Close one. I went inside and found Brittany at a table.

"Well?" she asked.

"Taken care of," I reported. "For now."

Eric Hayes passed our table, stopped, and turned back. He was a jock on the baseball team and friends with my ex-boyfriend, Jake Impenna.

"Hey, Mary-Kate," he said. "Saw you out there talking to Craig Withers. Looks like things are working out for you two, huh?" He grinned and walked away.

"What was that?" I asked Brittany. "Was he kidding?"

She shrugged. "The rumors won't stop until we stop Beauty or Beast," she said.

She was right. On the way home we stopped at Click for a latte. I couldn't resist checking

Beauty or Beast again. "I'll be right back," I told Brittany. She nodded and flipped through a magazine. I hurried to a computer terminal.

Had anyone written anything else about me and Craig? Had anyone noticed my Gooseberry cereal T-shirt?

I clicked on my name. My ranking came up.

I was down to 3.9. I was in the threes!

Comments. Any new comments? I scrolled down. There were three new ones. I started to read:

Saw Mary-Kate today. She really doesn't bother on the weekends, does she? Looks like she threw on the first thing she touched.

I'm with you. But make that the first thing she touched from elementary school.

You know what? Sometimes boring is the best you can do. Cargo pants and tanks aren't so bad.

Malcolm put a latte down next to me. I closed the site.

"Can I ask you something?" Malcolm said.

I nodded. I couldn't talk if I wanted to. The number 3.9 was pounding through my brain.

"Why are you wearing a string around your neck?" He gave it a tug.

"It's not a string, it's a candy—" Then I realized I'd eaten all the candy off my necklace. I'd been walking around wearing a dingy piece of string as jewelry.

That was it. It was time to take action. No more Miss Boring. I was going to be the most fashionable girl in school—and make those Beauty or Beast gossips eat their words.

chapter seven

Ashley honked the horn. "Hurry up, Mary-Kate!"

It was Monday morning, and Ashley was waiting for me in the car. I checked my outfit in the mirror one last time. My white jeans, white sandals, and, for a splashy new look, a sleeveless pink sequined top. Not something I'd normally wear to school. But I wasn't interested in *normal*.

I hurried to the car and got in.

"Finally," Ashley said. "I really want to find out who TurtleShell is today. We've got to find a way to close down the Beauty or Beast site."

She didn't say anything about my pink top. I sighed. Was my look still too boring?

I felt a little guilty. Here I was, paying attention to the site that was making Ashley crazy. I was just as bad as everyone else.

"We'll find TurtleShell," I promised. "My editorial comes out on the school Website today. Maybe that will help."

"I hope so," Ashley said.

Ashley parked in the school lot and we went inside the building.

"I feel like I'm living in a soap opera," Ashley said, glancing around. "Look over there."

Matt Anoki and Kristen Carson were making out in the alcove by the trophy case.

"Wow," I said. "Matt and Kristen. I didn't think they knew each other. I've never even seen them talking—until today."

"They aren't getting a lot of talking done now," Ashley said. "And over there—Janine Martel is wearing makeup. She's never worn makeup before. Not even on photo day."

"Trying out a little makeup isn't such a big deal, is it?" I asked.

"No," Ashley answered. "But it's sad if she's doing it because of some stupid comment she read on Beauty or Beast."

A rush of heat shot up the back of my neck. I plucked at my sequined top—which nobody seemed to be noticing.

"She might have just felt like a change," I said.

Charlie Evert walked by, reeking of cologne. You could have smelled him from a mile away.

"Hey girls," he said, clicking his tongue and waggling his eyebrows at us.

"Uh, hi, Charlie," I said, trying not to inhale.

"Whew!" Ashley exclaimed after Charlie Evert passed us. "I guess Charlie Evert just felt like pouring a bottle of cologne over himself. That must have something to do with Beauty or Beast."

"There *was* a comment about him smelling kind of mayonnaise-y," I said.

"See how the site has made everyone insecure and loony!" Ashley said. "I'm sure that somehow it's behind Matt and Kristen making out with each other in the hallway. I'm just not sure how. Plus Jared and Olivia's breakup, of course."

I sighed. I knew she was right. It was silly to change yourself because of the site. But I couldn't help wishing somebody would say something nice about my pink top. The sequins flashed in the bright school lights, but no one seemed to notice.

I guess changing my top wasn't enough, I thought. *Looks like I'll have to do something even more drastic.*

I headed to homeroom. I still felt like I was on

a soap set and not at my school. Especially when Mina Eng slapped Roger Gore about three feet away from me.

"How dare you!" she shouted. "You cretin!"

Cretin? I thought. Mina doesn't talk like that. Nobody does. Even her words sounded like a bad soap opera script.

"Hey, Ashley!"

I'd know that voice anywhere. I turned, already smiling. "Hi, Aaron."

My smile faded a little when I saw the sunburn on his cheeks. Had he gotten that sunburn wandering around the Santa Monica Pier with a blond girl who wasn't me?

Don't turn your own life into a soap opera, I warned myself.

"How was your weekend?" I asked. That was a totally normal question. Wasn't it?

"Great!" he answered. He looked straight into my eyes like he always did. He didn't seem to be hiding anything.

"What'd you end up doing on Saturday afternoon?" I asked. I winced. I hadn't meant to sound so suspicious. I hoped he didn't notice.

"Went to see *Aphid Power 4* with Will," he answered.

Mary-Kate and I had seen that movie just last week. I saw a window of opportunity open up and I jumped through it.

"Cool. Did you like it?" I twisted my ring around and around my finger. "I thought that scene where the aphid eats its way through Paris was amazing."

Aaron frowned. "Paris? The aphids don't eat Paris. Just New York, London, and Tokyo."

My ears started to burn. I couldn't believe I just tried to trick my boyfriend. I thought if he hadn't really seen the movie he would have just agreed the scene was great. I thought I could catch him in a lie.

"Oh, I must be thinking of *Attack of the Cockroaches,*" I said in a rush. "I should go. The bell's about to ring."

I hurried off before Aaron could say a word. *I'm as bad as everyone else at school,* I thought. *I'm letting Beauty or Beast turn me into somebody else! A person who doesn't trust her boyfriend!*

I froze. No. I wasn't going to let that happen.

I turned around. Aaron was gone. He'd disappeared into the crowd.

"Aaron!" I shouted as loud as I could. Heads turned, but I didn't care. "Aaron!" I yelled again.

Aaron stepped away from the drinking fountain about five feet away from me. "You called?" he asked. He wiped the droplets of water clinging to his mouth on the back of his hand.

I hurried over to him. " Aaron, I have a confession to make. I was testing you before. When I said that stupid thing about the aphid eating through Paris. I'm sorry."

He raised an eyebrow. "You wanted to see if I actually believed an aphid could swallow the Eiffel Tower?" he joked.

"No." My tongue glued itself to the top of my mouth. I knew I had to tell the truth. But it was hard. "No, I was trying to find out if you'd actually gone to the movie or not."

Aaron shook his head. "I don't get it. Why?"

I forced myself to look him in the eye. "Because on the Beauty or Beast site it said you were at the Santa Monica Pier on Saturday afternoon. With a girl. Not me, obviously," I explained.

"Oh."

That was it. Just *oh*.

"I guess if I read something like that about you, it would be hard to take," Aaron said.

"There was more stuff about you and other girls. I shouldn't have believed any of it, even for a second, and I didn't at first. But it kept creeping in," I said. "Do you forgive me?"

"Yeah. But next time don't try to trick me, just ask me," Aaron said.

"There won't be a next time, I swear," I promised him.

He pulled me into a hug and rested his chin on top of my head. I felt better—much better.

Then the bell rang.

"Bye," I said. But I didn't let go.

"Bye," he said. He didn't let go either.

"Bye," I said again, and this time I forced myself to pull away.

I slid into my seat a minute before the second bell.

Sarah Hunter took her seat half a second later.

"I saw you and Aaron in the hall," she whispered. "I'm glad you two aren't breaking up. It seems like every two feet some couple is breaking up. You guys are so good together."

She was right. And I'd come so close to messing things up!

Mr. Burkett started to take attendance. An aide from the office walked in and handed him a note.

"Ashley Olsen, you're wanted in the principal's office," Mr. Burkett announced. "Immediately."

I gulped. I'd never been called to the principal's office.

Was I in trouble?

chapter eight

All eyes were on me as I gathered my backpack. My knees felt like they were filled with cottage cheese when I stood up, but I managed to walk out into the hallway.

I made my way to the administration office. Mrs. Walsh, Principal Needham's secretary, gave me a sympathetic smile.

"Good morning, Ashley," she said. "Would you like a jelly bean?" She held out the jar filled with jelly beans that always sat on the corner of her desk.

"No thanks, Mrs. Walsh."

"We've missed you around here, Ashley," Mrs. Walsh said. "You were one of our best office workers when you were a sophomore."

"Thanks," I said.

"You can go on in," she told me. "The principal is expecting you."

My hand was icy cold when I pulled open the door to Principal Needham's office.

Principal Needham paced behind his desk, talking on the phone. He gestured me to a seat on the leather couch against the wall.

When I worked in the office, I liked coming in here. There's a basketball hoop in one corner, one of those electronic dartboards against the back of the door, and a mini bowling alley game on the desk. Principal Needham used to be a jock.

But today the office didn't seem as much fun. Why was I here? *Please just hang up and tell me!* I silently begged.

As if he'd heard me, Principal Needham ended his call.

I thought that's what I wanted. But then Principal Needham turned his complete attention on me. And the coldness in my hands spread through my entire body.

"That was *another* call about Beauty or Beast," Principal Needham told me. "All morning I've done nothing but take calls from parents about that Website."

He sat down, picked up a squishy plastic ball,

and started squeezing it. That's what he did when he was really stressed. It helped control his blood pressure.

"I took a look at the Website myself," Principal Needham said. *Squeeze, squeeze, squeeze.* "A long look. And I thought it was completely tasteless." *Squeeze, squeeze.*

I nodded. "I think so too, Mr. Needham," I said.

I completely agreed. But I still didn't understand why I was in the principal's office.

Principal Needham gave the ball a few more hard squeezes, then tossed it on his desk with a sigh.

"Ashley, I feel like I know you pretty well." He stared me directly in the eye. "I can't tell you how disappointed I am that you would have anything to do with such a terrible site."

I felt as if I'd been hit by a lightning bolt. I jumped to my feet.

"But I don't have anything to do with it!" I exclaimed. "I hate that site! I hate how much it's hurting people! You have to believe me!"

Suddenly I realized I was yelling at the principal. I sat down and folded my hands in my lap. I forced myself to speak in a low, calm voice.

"Someone stole the pictures for Beauty or Beast from my Love Link site," I explained. "And they used the same colors and type that I use on my site. But I have nothing to do with Beauty or Beast."

I leaned forward. Would he believe me?

Principal Needham rubbed his temples. "Maybe I didn't get enough facts. I should have investigated the situation before I started making accusations. I'm sorry."

"It's okay." I started to stand up again.

"But, Ashley, we have a problem, no matter who is behind Beauty or Beast," Principal Needham said.

I sank back down on the couch.

"This has made me rethink the whole Bayside High server policy." He rolled the stress ball across his desk. "I've decided that it's not appropriate for the school to host a matchmaking Website."

I opened my mouth to protest, but nothing came out.

Principal Needham rolled the stress ball in the other direction. It fell off the desk with a soft splat.

"So, starting tomorrow, Love Link will be

pulled off the school server," he said. "In fact, all school Websites will be pulled. Even the main Bayside High site."

I gasped. Mary-Kate would be crushed. And I hated to lose Love Link.

"At least for now, until we get everything cleaned up," Principal Needham added.

"But—" I started to say.

"I'm afraid I don't have time to discuss it now, Ashley." He stood up. "A group of parents will be here to talk about Beauty or Beast shortly. I need to prepare." He flicked his hand toward the door.

What could I do? I left the office.

chapter nine

"It's not fair!" Mary-Kate called through the closed bathroom door. "Mr. Needham can't close Love Link! And the school Website came out against Beauty or Beast!"

"I know," I said, leaning against the door. I stood in the hall outside the bathroom, waiting for Mary-Kate to come out. She'd been in there forever. What was she doing?

"We've got to find TurtleShell," I said. "If we can get him or her to confess to Mr. Needham, maybe that will make the parents happy. It might convince him that there's only one problem Website, and he'll let us bring back the rest."

"But we still have another problem," Mary-Kate said. "Someone is writing lies about you and me on that Website. I want to know who it is and why they're doing it. Maybe Malcolm can help."

"But how?" I asked. "It's all anonymous."

Mary-Kate was quiet for a minute.

"Mary-Kate?" I called.

"Aarrgh!" she screamed.

"Mary-Kate!" I banged on the locked door. "Open up! What's the matter?"

The bathroom door swung open.

I gasped. "What did you do to yourself?"

"I dyed my hair!" I wailed.

And the color—the color was nothing like the cool, vibrant red on the box. It was rusty orange in some places, Kool-Aid orange in others, with a few patches of my regular blond mixed in.

I was hideous! But this wasn't a pair of sweats I could yank off in a second. It was my hair!

"Oh, Mary-Kate, why?" Ashley exclaimed.

I took a deep breath and told the truth. I didn't want to keep this secret from my sister anymore.

"Beauty or Beast," I confessed. "There was a post that said I was boring. I know I shouldn't have cared. I know paying attention to anything on that site was stupid. I know—"

"You know you're just like most of the kids at school," Ashley interrupted. "Lots of people went

84

a little crazy after they read something on that site."

"Lots of people weren't writing articles about it," I reminded her. "They weren't going off about how mean-spirited and wrong the site was. They weren't trying to shut it down."

I stared down at my orange-stained hands. "How could I have cared about anything written on Beauty or Beast?"

"You should have seen me with Aaron this morning," Ashley told me. "I know I said that I didn't believe he was sneaking around with some other girl. And I really didn't believe it."

She reached out and took a section of my three-toned hair between her fingers. "But all I could think about was those posts. So I . . . I gave him a pop quiz."

"A pop quiz?" I repeated.

"Trying to trick him," Ashley explained. "I asked him questions about the movie he said he saw with his brother to see if he'd mess up. Things like that."

"He passed, I'm guessing," I said.

Ashley frowned at the section of hair. "Yeah, but he also found out what I was doing," she told me. "He could have been furious. He could have broken up with me. But he understood how what I read got to me."

"Like what I read got to me." I let out an enormous sigh. "It was as if I had a bunch of little people living in my head, talking about how boring I was. Well, when they weren't saying I was a Goody Two shoes. Or crazy about Craig Withers."

"We've got to stop this. But first we've got to do something about your hair." Ashley pushed past me into the bathroom. She grabbed the empty box of dye off the sink and started to read the back.

"Well?" I asked.

"Luckily you picked a temporary dye," she told me. "It's supposed to wash out in a day or two."

"A day or two!" I cried. "You mean I have to go to school looking like a mangled Raggedy Ann doll? What am I going to do?"

Ashley shrugged. "Got any hats?"

❀

"Mary-Kate, oh wow! What a great hat," Lauren squealed when Mary-Kate and I walked into the cafeteria the next day.

"Thanks," she said. "I've been trying to hide out all day, but I decided it's time to come out and face my public." She tugged her floppy white hat off.

"Look," she said.

Her hair was still a bright, patchy orange.

Brittany gave a low whistle. "Nasty," she said.

"Just more damage caused by the Beauty or Beast Website," I said. "We've got work to do. We've got to figure out who TurtleShell is—today."

"TurtleShell. Huh. Who would choose the screen name TurtleShell?" Lauren asked.

Brittany popped a cherry tomato from her salad into her mouth. "What about reptile boy?"

"Bob McSweeney?" Mary-Kate said. "The guy with the snakes?"

Bob McSweeney was one of my Love Link failures. He refused to go anywhere without his pet snakes. Most girls didn't appreciate it.

"But aren't turtles amphibians?" Lauren asked.

"Hello? Grade-school science, anyone?" Brittany said. "If it lays gelatinous eggs in water, it's an amphibian. Hence, a turtle is a reptile. And reptile boy likes reptiles. So his screen name could be TurtleShell."

I pulled out my purple glitter notebook and flipped it open to a blank page. I started a list of possible Beauty or Beast Webmasters with Bob McSweeney's name on top.

"But even though turtles *are* reptiles, I don't think they are Bob's kind of reptiles," Lauren said. "Snakes just seem way different to me. I bet there are turtle guys and snake guys. Just like skater guys and surfer guys."

I wrote Lauren's theory down in my notebook. If I was going to find the Webmaster, I needed to consider everything. "If not Bob, who?"

"What about Michael Gelb?" Mary-Kate suggested. "He's obsessed with that band the Glow Turtles. Maybe that's where the TurtleShell name comes from."

"Hmmm." I wrote the name down. "Aaron and I were doing a profile of what we thought the Webmaster would be like. We kind of thought he or she wouldn't have a girlfriend or boyfriend."

"I can see that," Brittany said. "If you're happy with someone, do you really care about ranking everyone at school and gossiping about who is with whom?"

"Well, Michael has been going out with a girl from Westwood," I said. "That doesn't absolutely mean he's *not* our guy."

"Michael is so into the Glow Turtles, I doubt he

would have time to work on a Website," Brittany added. "Like Mary-Kate said, he's obsessed."

"Maybe Rebecca Antrim?" Lauren suggested. "She actually gets paid to do Websites for people."

Mary-Kate licked the last of her raspberry yogurt off her spoon. "So why waste time doing a site like Beauty or Beast instead of making cash?"

Lauren nodded.

"I've got it!" Brittany snapped her fingers. "What about Gene Stanley? He's practically a computer *genius*. He'd be able to get a site like Beauty or Beast up and running in a flash."

I tapped my pen on my notebook. "Gene always seems so nice. I can't really see him wanting to cause so much trouble at school."

"Well . . . maybe he didn't think it would cause trouble," Mary-Kate said. She scraped her spoon around and around in her yogurt carton even though it was empty.

I stared at her in surprise. "Rating people as beauties or beasts is mean no matter what," I said. "And anyway, once he saw what was happening around school, the Webmaster, whoever he or she is, could have taken the site down. But they didn't."

"You're right," Mary-Kate answered, looking down at her tray.

"I say you should put Gene on the list," Brittany urged. "He seems nice, but how well do any of us really know him? Plus he's always helping out in the computer lab. That means he has access to all the school servers."

I added Gene's list to my name.

"Gene seems our most likely candidate so far—because of the school-server thing." I smiled at Brittany. "You're going to have to be the one to get more info about him," I teased. "He has such a crush on you."

Brittany wrinkled her nose. Then she sighed. "Anything to save Ashley's reputation," Brittany said.

I slapped my hands down on the table. "It's time to plan Operation Takedown TurtleShell!"

chapter ten

"We'll be able to hear everything from here," I told Lauren. We were huddled in the hall around the corner from Gene's locker. Brittany waited at the other end of the hall.

"Remember the plan," I said to Lauren. "When Gene goes to his locker, Brittany follows him."

"Right," Lauren said. "She gets him to confess somehow—" *We hadn't exactly figured that part out yet*. "—and we're the witnesses."

"Right," I said.

Lauren peeked around the corner. "No sign of him yet, Ashley. Oooh, wait!" She pulled back and pressed herself against the wall. "He's coming down the hall!"

Lauren took another peek.

"Don't be too obvious," I warned.

Lauren ducked back. "Brittany's on his tail," she whispered.

We heard a *thunk*.

"Shhh. I think Brittany just did the drop-the-binder thing." I inched a tiny bit closer to the corner and listened hard.

"Thanks, Gene," I heard Brittany say.

"No problem," Gene said. "Great sticker. Do you like turtles?"

"Do you like turtles?" Gene asked.

"Mary-Kate's a genius," I whispered to Lauren.

Mary-Kate had come up with the idea to slap a turtle sticker on Brittany's binder to give Gene an easy conversation starter. Brittany complained a little. She thought the sticker looked silly. But Mary-Kate promised she'd scrape it off for her post-plan.

I tuned back to Gene and Brittany's conversation.

"So we were having this whole argument about amphibians and reptiles," Brittany was saying.

"You were absolutely right, and your friend was absolutely wrong," Gene was saying.

Lauren elbowed me. "I know already," she whispered.

"Shhh . . ." I put my finger to my lips.

"A single scientific discipline does cover both amphibians and reptiles," Gene continued.

"Herpetology, right?" Brittany said.

"When is she going to get his E-mail address?" Lauren twisted her hands together. "She doesn't have all day."

"Right!" Gene answered.

I could tell he was smiling just from his voice. Brittany was doing great.

"They probably got lumped together at some point because—" Gene went on.

"I'm thinking of getting a turtle for a pet," Brittany interrupted.

Yay, Brittany! I thought. She managed to get back to the script we came up with at lunch.

"Really? Cool," Gene said. "I have five turtles myself, all different species."

The bell rang.

"Oh, gotta go," Gene told Brittany.

"I'd love to have your help picking the right kind of turtle," Brittany said quickly. "Do you think I could have your E-mail address?"

"Sure!" Gene exclaimed.

I could hear the smile in his voice again.

"It's TurtleShell."

Lauren and I leaped around the corner.

"It's you!" I yelled. "You're TurtleShell!"

Gene whirled to face me.

I pointed at him. "You're the Webmaster for the Beauty or Beast site."

"Don't try to deny it," Lauren told him. "We know TurtleShell runs the site."

Gene backed away a step. "I've got to get to class." He backed up another step—and bumped into Brittany.

"Oh, no, you don't," Brittany said.

"You're going to Principal Needham's office with Ashley," Lauren informed him. "All the school Websites were shut down because your site got all the parents upset. You're going to confess."

"Yeah," I added. "And then maybe we can get the other sites back."

Lauren and Brittany left for class while I led Gene to Mr. Needham's office.

"I'm sorry about the other Websites," Gene said. "I didn't know."

"Why did you do it anyway?" I asked.

"It was just supposed to be a joke. For me and my friends. No one else was even supposed to see it," he told me.

"How is it a joke to rate people? Would you

think it was funny if you went on line and saw that everyone at school thought you were a total beast?" I demanded.

Gene blinked. "Do they?"

"That's not the point." I sighed. "You hurt people's feelings. Couples broke up because of you. Friends got into fights."

"People said nice things too," he protested. But his voice came out soft and weak.

"Not very many of them," I answered.

"Oh," Gene said. He was quiet for a minute. Then he looked up at me. "I know I should have shut it down myself. It's just that my friends got all psyched that this private joke became the hottest thing at school."

He started walking. "I really didn't mean for all this to happen. It just got out of control so fast."

"I believe you," I said.

Gene hesitated right outside the office door. "I really do think Brittany would like a turtle. She's really cool, and so are turtles. I'm not talking about in the clammy way," he added quickly. "If she ever wants to talk to me again, I'll tell her the best kind to get."

"Okay," I said.

"I always kind of wanted to use your Love

Link site myself," he told me. "I hoped maybe it would match me up with her."

"Maybe Principal Needham will let all the other student sites back on line. Then you can try it out," I said. "Not that I can give you any promises about Brittany."

We stepped into the outer office and I told Mrs. Walsh that we needed to see Principal Needham. She buzzed him, then told us to go in.

Mr. Needham held up a finger. "Final shot of the game," he told us. He threw a Nerf ball at the basketball hoop. *Swish!*

"Yes!" he cried.

Mr. Needham was definitely in a better mood today. The stress ball was nowhere in sight.

"Pull up a couch," he said. "What can I do for you?"

Gene and I sat down. "I did it. I hijacked Ashley's Website to create the Beauty or Beast Website," he blurted out.

Suddenly Principal Needham's happy expression drained off his face. He sat down. "Go on."

"I copied kids' pictures from her site. I used her basic design and colors too. It was fast and easy. And I wasn't planning for a lot of people to see it," Gene explained. "I guess someone saw it while they were surfing around and—it just exploded."

"It certainly exploded," Principal Needham said. "You should have seen the parents I met with yesterday. They were very upset. And I understand. Who wouldn't be if their child was labeled a beast?"

Gene nodded. He slunk down in his seat.

"Who wouldn't be if lies were told about their child?" Mr. Needham continued.

Gene nodded again. He seemed to be disappearing deeper into the sofa.

"Ashley, I'd like you to leave us alone while we discuss what disciplinary action is suitable for Gene and his friends," Mr. Needham said.

I couldn't get out of there fast enough. I didn't want to watch Gene's punishment. He really did seem to be sorry for what he'd done.

I started for the door. Then I turned back. "Oh, Mr. Needham, I was wondering. . . does this mean Love Link—and the other student sites— will get back on line?"

"I told you, Ashley, I don't think a matchmaking site should be sponsored by the school," Mr. Needham said. "And that's what being on the school server means. Beyond that, I want to check all the sites myself before I'll allow them back on the server."

"But people love Love Link," I protested.

"They do, really," Gene volunteered.

I smiled at Gene, but he wasn't exactly the person I wanted on my side right now. Still, I knew he was only trying to help.

"Tons of people use it. And there are lots of happy couples at Bayside because of it," I said.

"I don't disagree with that, Ashley," Principal Needham told me. "I think it's a fine site—for a public server."

"But—"

Principal Needham held up a hand to stop me.

"I'm not singling you out," he said. "I'm restricting the school server to official school organizations with a teacher sponsor. It's become very clear that the Websites need much more supervision."

"So the school Website can come back?" I asked.

"Yes," he said. *At least Mary-Kate would be happy about that.* "But not Love Link."

The principal opened his desk drawer and pulled out his stress ball. "I'm sure"—*squeeze,*

squeeze—"you understand that." *Squeeze, squeeze, squeeze.*

"Yes," I replied.

I *did* understand.

But I also believed, deep in my heart of hearts, that Love Link could be saved.

The question was how?

chapter eleven

"Um, Mary-Kate?" a quavery voice said the next day. I closed my locker and turned around. Craig Withers stood there, nervously twisting his hands together. "I need to talk to you again."

Uh-oh. I hoped he wasn't going to suggest more sneaking around behind his mother's back. "What is it?" I asked.

"I want to apologize," he said.

Apologize? "For what?" I asked.

"For being a jerk," he said. "For believing those rumors about us on Beauty or Beast."

"That's okay," I said. "But—how did you find out they weren't true?"

"Well, I had a feeling when I talked to you at the mall the other day that you were just being nice to me. I mean, I could tell you didn't really want to go to the mechanical physics convention with me."

"Go on." At least Craig was getting something out of this. Every time he spoke to me, he seemed a little less nervous.

"So I decided to investigate a little and find out who started those rumors," he said. "I don't know if you realize this, but people don't pay much attention to me. I mean, they don't really notice when I'm around. It's very good for eavesdropping."

My eyebrows shot up. "And you heard something interesting?"

He nodded. "I heard Alexis Byrne talking to one of her friends about Aaron. She used exactly the same words that someone used on Beauty or Beast. So I hacked into the Website and found the name of the person who posted those comments about Aaron and Ashley. The screen name was *alexisb*."

"You're kidding!" I gasped. Why hadn't we guessed it? Alexis had a crush on Aaron—she even tried to steal him from Ashley. So of course she'd try to break them up.

"She posted the rumors about us, too," Craig told me. "I guess she doesn't like you and your sister very much."

I laughed and threw my arms around him. "Thank you, Craig! Thank you so much! You helped us solve the mystery!"

I couldn't wait to tell Ashley. But the bell rang and I had to go to my next class. I gave Craig another hug and said, "I owe you one. You want to meet for pizza later?"

"Uh, yeah," he said, pushing his glasses up his nose. "Except I can't eat cheese. I'm lactose-intolerant."

"Well, we'll do something else then," I said. "Something nondairy." I ran to class, leaving him standing there, stunned but happy.

I felt a tap on my shoulder in social studies later that day. I turned around slightly—I didn't want Ms. Hahn to see—and Bart Weinberg handed me a note with *Mary-Kate* written on the front.

I knew it was from Lauren. She always uses bright yellow paper. Not exactly the best choice for stealth note-passing, but *so* Lauren, Miss Cheerful.

Ms. Hahn's voice grew louder, and I realized she was walking down my row. I slid the slip of paper into my lap and frantically started taking notes on Ms. Hahn's lecture.

Democracy—what the majority of people want,

I scribbled. *What ways can the people show the government what they want? Voting. Protests. Letters to representatives. Petitions.*

Ms. Hahn passed by. I opened Lauren's note and scanned it: *We've got to do something about Ashley! She's miserable!*

Lauren was right. Ashley was really upset. She'd put in a zillion hours on Love Link. And now it was shut down. We'd found out who started Beauty or Beast—but that still didn't save Love Link. It looked hopeless.

I looked down at my notes. The words seemed to leap out at me. *Voting. Protests. Letters to representatives. Petitions.*

The inside of my head was beginning to itch.

Oh, yeah! I had an idea! A brilliant idea on how to save Love Link!

"Hey, Ash! Where have you been?" I asked my sister. She looked so sad.

"Over at Click," she told me. "Michelle Simmons apologized to me. I guess the word is out about Gene being the Beauty or Beast Webmaster, not me."

She flopped down on my bed. That was a bad sign. I'm the flopper in the family.

"That's good, isn't it?" I said.

"I guess." She sighed. "I met up with Malcolm on his break. But even the boy genius couldn't come up with any ideas for changing Principal Needham's mind."

"I did!" I exclaimed. "But first I have some big news. I know for sure that Aaron is not cheating on you."

She sat up. "How do you know?"

"Because Alexis posted those rumors!" I told her. "Craig Withers found out. She wrote about him and me, too."

"Alexis! I should have known," Ashley said. "Of course! She was so mean to Malcolm. And now this!"

Alexis tried to use Malcolm to get close to Aaron. And for a while, Malcolm actually liked her. Luckily, he got over her quickly.

"So you can stop worrying about Aaron and focus on saving Love Link," I said.

"I wasn't worried," she insisted. But I knew that wasn't true. "So what's your plan?"

"All we have to do is start a petition to save Love Link. Then we give it to Principal Needham, and your site is saved!"

"Do you really think we can get enough signatures to make Principal Needham change his mind?"

"Are you kidding? Of course we can," I told her. "Now everyone knows you had nothing to do with Beauty or Beast, so that's not a problem. You know every single happy couple you've gotten together would sign. And all the kids who like trying out new matches on your site."

Ashley sat up. "That's a lot of people right there."

"And all your friends would sign," I said. "Plus all the people who have wanted to try Love Link but haven't yet. I know there are people like that out there. Gene, for one."

Ashley grinned. "This really might work, Mary-Kate."

"Of course it will!" I answered. "Especially because the lead story on tomorrow's Web page is going to be all about why Love Link should be saved!"

"Really?" Ashley cried.

"Yup. I turned it in before I left school," I answered.

Someone knocked on the door.

"Come in," I called.

I grinned as Brittany and Lauren bustled in carrying cartons of Thai food.

"What's going on?" Ashley asked.

"It's the Save Love Link petition committee," I told her.

"The carton with the red X is the mild curry, which is still hot enough to burn your tongue," Brittany announced. She took a seat on my floor.

Lauren handed out cans of soda and napkins.

Ashley pulled out her notebook. "Okay, guys, let's plan. We don't have a lot of time."

"We should start with the couples you got together," I said. "Why don't you E-mail them all tonight and give them a heads-up about the petition? I'm sure they'll all want to sign."

"Great idea." Ashley wrote it down.

"We should print the petition on bright colored paper," Lauren suggested. "That way it will be easy for people to spot."

"Why don't we each carry a copy of the petition?" Brittany added. "We have a lot of territory to cover. Four of us can get the signatures four times as fast."

"Great, great," Ashley said. Then she looked up from her notebook and smiled at all of us. "We really are going to save Love Link, aren't we?"

❀

"Sign the petition!" I shouted the next day

after school. "Keep Ashley's Love Link alive!"

The quad was teeming with kids.

Two arms slipped around my waist the next day after school. A hand plucked my pen out of my fingers. I twisted my head back and saw Aaron smiling down at me.

I smiled back. "Hey! What are you doing?"

"I'm signing your petition, Ashley." He rested his chin on the top of my head. I held my clipboard steady while he signed.

"I'm very in favor of Love Link. That's how I met you," he reminded me. Then he turned me toward him and kissed me.

"It wasn't Love Link yet," I told him when we broke apart. "It was when I had the matchmaking service at Click."

"I know that. But it was the Theory of Compatibility. And it was created by you. So I think that counts."

"I think so, too." I wished I could stand there with him all day.

"Um, I want to sign the petition—if that's okay," someone said behind me.

I whirled around. Aaron grunted as I accidentally knocked him in the stomach with my clipboard. Gene stood there, staring at his feet.

"Of course you can sign," I told him.

I knew he felt bad. And I needed every signature I could get! I held out the petition.

Gene hesitated. "Don't other people have petitions too?" he asked.

"Yes, but this one is—" Then I got it. He had a special petition-carrier in mind. "Mary-Kate has a petition at the north entrance. And Lauren is at the south," I teased.

I knew exactly who he was looking for.

"Oh, okay." Gene started away. He moved as slowly as one of his turtles.

"And Brittany's over at the door by the gym," I added.

Gene yelled a thank-you and raced off.

"What was that about?" Aaron asked.

"Don't you recognize a crush when you see it?" I asked.

"Not as quickly as you do," he answered. "Uh-oh, look who is coming this way."

I followed his gaze. Alexis Byrne was heading toward us.

"Hey, Alexis!" Aaron called. "Aren't you going to sign Ashley's petition?"

She didn't answer. She veered away from us and started walking faster.

"Oh, that's right! You're a Beauty or Beast fan!" Aaron called after her.

I'd told Aaron about the source of those rumors. I couldn't believe I'd let Alexis upset me so much.

"I've got to go," Aaron said. "Soccer practice. I'll call you tonight to find out the totals on the signatures."

"Bye," I called after him.

It's silly, but I always feel a little lonely after he leaves me. Even when I'm surrounded by people. *You've got work to do,* I reminded myself.

"Sign the petition! Save Love Link!" I shouted. I waved the petition over my head.

Jared-and-Olivia wandered over and signed. They were back to being a single creature with one name again. Everyone at school now knew Beauty or Beast was a bunch of lies. At least the truth flies as fast as rumors at this school some of the time. Everyone also knew I had nothing to do with Beauty or Beast.

"How's it going?" Diane Challem ran over and pulled the petition out of my fingers. Rick Storace was right behind her. Diane and Rick were almost always together, thanks to Love Link!

"You have almost twice as many signatures as

you did at lunch," Rick said. "That's great!"

"I wish we could sign twice," Diane said. "Here, at least touch my bracelet for luck. It has jade in it. Jade is very lucky."

I touched one of the jade beads. "Thanks. Now Love Link will have to get back on line," I told her.

"Without a doubt." She handed me back the petition. "See you later. We're off to King Kone."

"Have fun." It's so cool seeing couples Love Link has gotten together.

And two more came—Veronica Deaver and Barry Sommerfield. My Theory of Compatibility was right on target with them.

"Hey, we found you," Barry called.

"We saw Mary-Kate, but we really wanted to sign your petition," Veronica added as they hurried up to me.

"We know it's the same, but, you know, you're the one who really got us together," Barry said.

"Thanks, you guys," I said as they added their names. My sheet was getting really full.

I cleared my throat and raised the petition over my head again. "Sign the petition! Save Love Link!" I cried.

The after-school crowd was thinning out. I

scanned the quad and saw Mary-Kate heading toward me.

"Time to tally," Mary-Kate announced when she reached me.

I checked my watch. She was right. It had gotten to be five o'clock so fast!

I sat down on the nearest bench. Mary-Kate plopped down next to me.

"Here come Brittany and Lauren," I said.

They took the bench across from me and Mary-Kate, and we all started to count signatures.

I started tapping my toes when I was halfway down the list. I couldn't help it. This was exciting. There were a *lot* of names!

"Two hundred and six!" Brittany announced.

"A hundred and eighty-four!" Lauren cried.

"Two hundred and five!" Mary-Kate exclaimed.

I took a deep breath. "Three hundred and seventeen!"

"You broke three hundred! Wow!" Mary-Kate yelled.

We all high-fived, even though we pretty much gave that up years ago.

"So, grand total." I closed my eyes and did some fast addition. "Ladies, today we gathered nine hundred and twelve votes!"

"That's about, hmm, ninety-five percent of the school!" Brittany let out a whoop.

"Democracy in action," Mary-Kate cried. "This has got to work."

But a high school isn't really a democracy, I thought. It all came down to Principal Needham. All that mattered was what he thought.

And I had to wait until tomorrow to find that out.

chapter twelve

"So, Principal Needham, that's *nine hundred and twelve* signatures," I said firmly. "And, as I'm sure you know, nine hundred and twelve signatures represents more than ninety-five percent of the students of Bayside High."

I stood up a little straighter.

"It's very clear that the majority of people at school want Ashley's Love Link back on the school server," I continued. "It's your decision. What do you say?"

"Ashley, if you still want a ride with me, we have to leave now," Mom called.

"Coming," I called back, wishing I had time to rehearse my speech to the principal once more—even though I'd been standing in front of the bathroom mirror for an hour, pretending to talk to him.

I grabbed my backpack, unzipped it, and counted the petitions to make sure all four were inside. Of course, I'd counted them last night when I'd put them in. But I wanted to double-check everything. My meeting with Principal Needham had to go perfectly.

"Ashley!" Mom called again.

I hurried to the kitchen and we headed out to the car. I wanted to get to school early so the principal would absolutely have time to see me before my first class. Mom said she'd drop me off on her way to the day-care center she runs. Mary-Kate was coming later in the Mustang.

"Nervous?" Mom asked as she pulled out of the driveway.

"A little," I answered. Then I told the truth. Why keep secrets from Mom? "So nervous I can barely remember how to breathe."

Mom laughed. "You're going to be great. I know firsthand how persuasive you can be. When you were seven, you came to me and your dad with a list of reasons why you should never have to eat tuna again. It even included a list of equally good alternate sources of protein."

"I like tuna now," I said.

"But for a year and a half you didn't touch the

stuff, and I didn't try to make you. You convinced me," Mom answered. "And I'm much harder to win over than Principal Needham."

I smiled at her. "That's so not true. Principal Needham is a nice guy. But he never likes to look too soft in front of the students."

Mom pulled into the school parking lot. "Okay, maybe not. But no matter what happens today, you can know you've tried your hardest. That's what matters."

"Thanks." I climbed out of the car and marched straight to the principal's office. Before I stepped into the outer office I pulled out my folder of petitions. Then I lifted my chin, stuck a smile on my face, and opened the door.

"Good morning, Ashley," Mrs. Walsh said.

"Hi." My fake smile turned real. It's impossible not to smile at Mrs. Walsh.

"Jelly bean?" she asked, tilting the jar on her desk toward me.

"Not right now, thanks," I answered. "I wondered if I could talk to Principal Needham for a minute."

"I'm sorry, sweetie. The principal is preparing to present our budget to the school superintendent," Mrs. Walsh told me. "The poor man is barely going to have time to blow his nose today."

"I don't need more than two minutes," I assured her. "I timed myself."

"I wish I could get you in there, but I just can't. Are you sure you sure you don't want a jelly bean?" Mrs. Walsh rattled the glass jar again.

"No thanks."

The office door suddenly opened and Mr. Needham popped his head out.

"Oh—Ashley, you're in luck," Mrs. Walsh said. "Here he is."

"Hi, Ashley," Mr. Needham said. "What's up?"

I waved the petitions at him. "Almost everyone in school has signed these petitions, Mr. Needham," I said. "To reinstate Love Link. Would you please look at them?"

He shook his head. "I'm sorry, Ashley. I don't have time to look at them today. And I don't need to see them—I've already made up my mind. I'm afraid a petition can't change it."

"But Mr. Needham—" I pleaded.

"Sorry, Ashley—I'm swamped today. Can I get that file, Mrs. Walsh?" He disappeared into his office.

Mrs. Walsh stood up and went to the file cabinet. "I'm sorry, dear. He just doesn't have time today."

"Can I make an appointment to see him when he's not so busy?" I said. "I've got to show him these petitions. I just know that when he sees all these names . . ."

"One second, Ashley." She pulled a file from the drawer and took it into Mr. Needham's office. Then she came back, sat at her desk, and looked at her appointment calendar.

"How's Friday?" she asked.

"But that's two days away!" I protested.

"Sorry. Best I can do," Mrs. Walsh said.

"I'll take it," I said. "I'll change his mind. You'll see."

"I'm on your side, dear," Mrs. Walsh said. "I always liked that Love Link site."

Too bad, I thought. *Because it looks like Love Link is doomed.*

"So?" Mary-Kate asked me after school that day. "What did Mr. Needham think of the petitions? Did all our hard work pay off?"

"He doesn't even have time to look at them until Friday," I said. "And he said he's made up his mind already."

Mary-Kate frowned. "I can't believe it. There's got to be a way around this. What are you going to do ?"

I shrugged. "What can I do? Normally I'd work on Love Link. I guess I'll just go home. Are you going to the Website office?"

Mary-Kate nodded, and then her face lit up. "Why don't you come with me?" she said. "I've got an idea."

She dragged me down the hall to the Website office. "Wait here," she said, and disappeared inside Ms. Barbour's office. A few minutes later the door opened and she came out.

"Ms. Barbour has something to tell you," she announced.

I went into the office. Ms. Barbour smiled at me. "Ashley, let me go to your meeting with Mr. Needham on Friday. I think I can convince him to bring back Love Link."

"But how?" I asked.

"He's allowing sites that have teacher sponsors," Mary-Kate reminded me.

"And I'd be delighted to sponsor Love Link," Ms. Barbour said. "It started here at the main school Website anyway. What do you think?"

"That's fantastic!" I said. "Thank you, Ms. Barbour!" I stopped myself from jumping up and down for joy. But I knew this would work. Love Link was coming back! I couldn't wait!

• • •

"I think this is an important issue, Ed," Ms. Barbour said on Friday afternoon.

Mary-Kate, Ms. Barbour, and I were sitting in Mr. Needham's office. Mr. Needham seemed surprised to see Ms. Barbour with us. The signed petitions sat in front of him on his desk.

Mr. Needham scanned the petitions. "I know Ashley's worked very hard on Love Link," he said. "But I'm still not convinced it's appropriate."

"That's why I'm here," Ms. Barbour said. "Ashley monitors the content of the site very carefully. I have complete confidence in her. So I've volunteered to sponsor the site. I'll oversee the content and make sure nothing inappropriate is posted. Even though I trust Ashley completely."

Mr. Needham frowned. "It's not that I don't trust her. But Beauty or Beast was such a nightmare! Once the parents decide they don't like something, they don't back down until they get their way. I don't want to go through that again."

"But Love Link is nothing like Beauty or Beast," I protested. "There's no rating or meanness. It's more like a unique way for people to express themselves."

"The students really want Love Link back,"

Mary-Kate added. "Just look at all those signatures!"

Mr. Needham nodded. "It *is* very impressive. And I can see how much it means to you." He paused. "All right. Ms. Barbour, as long as you're willing to sponsor the site, Love Link can come back on line."

I broke into a broad grin and gripped Mary-Kate's hand to keep from cheering out loud.

"Thanks, Mr. Needham," I said. I stood up and shook his hand. "You won't regret it. I promise!"

"We did it!" Mary-Kate gave me a big hug. "We stopped Beauty or Beast and brought back Love Link!"

We gathered our friends in our backyard later that day for a Love Link celebration. Lauren, Brittany, Aaron, and Malcolm were there. Even Craig Withers showed up. His mother dropped him off. I was tempted to invite Gene, but Brittany said the turtle he gave her could act as his representative. She'd had enough of him for a while.

"You saved the kids of Bayside High from becoming a churning mass of gossips, liars, and back-stabbers," Malcolm said. "Hey, come to think of it—bring back Beauty or Beast!"

I glared at him.

"Just kidding, of course," he added.

"Thanks to all of you for your help," I said. "We couldn't have done it without you."

And it was true. All our friends had rallied to help us out. Lauren and Brittany helped with the petitions, and Brittany got Gene to confess to being the Beauty or Beast Webmaster. Malcolm found out Gene's screen name, and Craig figured out that Alexis was spreading nasty rumors about us. Mary-Kate had a million great ideas and got Ms. Barbour to sponsor Love Link. And Aaron supported me all the way.

Mary-Kate passed around a plate of sandwiches. Aaron handed me a glass of lemonade and leaned close to whisper in my ear.

"Congratulations," he said softly. "I knew you could do it. Quack quack quack."

"Quack quack" was like a secret code between us. Aaron liked to tease me about it.

I smiled and whispered back, "Quack to you, too."

"Hey," Mary-Kate said. "What are you two whispering about? I thought we weren't keeping secrets anymore."

"It's okay, Mary-Kate," I said. "We're not gossiping. It's just that some things are private."

Aaron put his arm around me. "I like you a lot, Ashley," he whispered. "And that's no secret."

"You're doing it again!" Mary-Kate protested. "Stop that!"

But she smiled at us, just teasing. And I was glad. Because as long as he was whispering nice things, I never wanted it to stop.

Find out what happens next in

Book 11:
Little White Lies

"Check this picture out," I said to my sister Ashley. I slid a photograph of our cousin Jeanine across the dining room table. "Her high school junior prom, remember?"

Mom decided to make a photo collage of Jeanine through the years for her wedding shower. So Ashley and I were going through a bunch of old albums and picking the best ones.

"Look, Mary-Kate!" Ashley said, sliding an album over for me to see. "Our famous three-family camping trip to Sequoia National Park! Remember that?"

"It's burned into my memory forever," I said, checking out the pictures.

Eight years ago, our family, Jeanine's family, and another family, the Harrises, had gone on a week-long camping trip together. It would have been perfect, except for . . .

"George!" I cried. I pointed to a photo of an eight-year-old boy. He was the same age as Ashley and me. His yellow-blond hair flopped over his forehead and his small blue eyes squinted against the sun. "Obnoxious George Harris!"

"He was awful, wasn't he?" Ashley said. "Remember the pine cones in our sleeping bags?"

"I remember everything he did to us," I said. "Chasing us with that fake snake, dunking us in the lake, griping about everything, and those horrible temper tantrums—" I broke off and took a deep breath. "He was the biggest pest I ever met!"

"I know," Ashley said. "I couldn't stand him either. "Hey, I wonder if he'll be at the wedding?"

"Don't even think it," I said with a shudder.

"We haven't seen him in years," she said. "Maybe he's changed by now."

"I'm sure he has," I agreed. "For the worse!"

The doorbell rang and a few seconds later, Jeanine stuck her head around the dining room door. She smiled at Ashley and me. "Hi, you guys! Your dad told me you were in here."

"Hey, it's the bride-to-be!" I said, smiling back at our cousin as she came over to the table. She looked great, as usual, her green eyes twinkling with excitement.

"Want to see some pictures of you that we picked for the photo collage?" Ashley asked.

"Sure!" Jeanine tossed a stiff sheet of poster board onto the table and sat down. "It's so great of Aunt Janet to host the shower for me."

"Mom loves doing it," I told her. I pointed to one of the photos. "Look, there you are winning some kind of prize."

Jeanine glanced at it. "That was the seventh grade speech prize. Look at those braces!" she groaned.

"They gave your smile a real sparkle," I teased.

"Is that the seating chart?" Ashley asked, pointing to Jeanine's poster board. Colored nametags were stuck all over it.

"Right, for the wedding reception," Jeanine said. "It's almost finished, but I want to check with Aunt Janet about where to put a couple of her friends. That's why I stopped by."

"She's on the phone," I said, pointing toward the kitchen. "Want me to tell her you're here?"

Jeanine shook her head. "I've been so busy since we moved the wedding date up, I'm going to sit still while I have the chance."

"Mary-Kate, look!" Ashley said. She turned the seating chart around and pointed to a name.

"George Harris," I read. "Oh, no! Please don't tell me he's at our table."

"George Harris?" Mom asked, coming in from the kitchen. "What a coincidence! That was his mother on the phone. We were just talking about him."

She gave Jeanine a kiss on the cheek hello and smiled at me. "Guess what, Mary-Kate?"

"What?" I asked.

"Mrs. Harris told me that George doesn't have a date for the wedding. And when she found out you were planning to go by yourself—"

A warning bell went off in my head. This didn't sound good . . .

"—she said wouldn't it be fun if the two of you went together," Mom continued. "I told Mrs. Harris you'd be happy to. So now you have a date for the wedding after all!"

"You *what*?" I cried. "Mom! How could you do that without even asking me?"

"George just got back from boarding school and he doesn't know anyone out here," Mom said. "And you don't have a boyfriend at the moment, right? So this is the perfect solution!"

My stomach sank as Mom took George's name-tag and stuck it next to mine.

"Mom, wait!" I said. "George can't be my date because...I have a new boyfriend!"

Ashley's eyebrows shot up and her mouth dropped open.

"You do?" Mom asked. "Why haven't you told me about him?" Mom asked.

"Oh, well, we just met," I said.

"That's wonderful," Mom said. "Who is he? What's his name?"

"Yeah, who's the lucky guy?" Jeanine asked.

Good question, I thought.

"Billy," I said, blurting out the first name that popped into my head.

"What's he like?" Mom asked.

"Oh, he's . . . cute. And smart," I added. "He's captain of the debate team."

This was kind of fun, actually. Since Billy didn't exist, I could make him anything I wanted. "And he likes to rock climb and he totally loves acoustic guitar."

"When can we meet him?" Mom asked.

"Ummm . . . soon," I said.

The phone rang. "That must be Katherine," Mom said, checking her watch. "She said she'd call. Come on, Jeanine, let's get this seating chart finished—once and for all!"

The second Mom and Jeanine were out of earshot, Ashley leaned across the table. "What do you think you're doing?" she asked. "There's no rock-climbing debater named Billy!"

"Shhh!" I glanced toward the kitchen door. "I know it was a lie, but I was desperate! Besides, Mom doesn't ever have to know. I've got it all figured out already."

"What do you mean?" Ashley whispered.

"I'll keep pretending that I have a boyfriend, right up until the wedding," I said. "That will give George plenty of time to find another date. Then, on the morning of the wedding, I'll tell Mom that Billy and I broke up. I'll be in the clear and nobody will be hurt by my little white lie."

"Good news, Mary-Kate!" Mom said, coming back

into the dining room with Jeanine. "I checked the plans for the shower and there's room for one more person. You can invite Billy!"

I gulped. "To the wedding shower?"

Mom nodded. "It's co-ed, so the whole family can meet him!"

"Uhhh, sure." I pasted on a smile. Now what was I going to do?

I hadn't planned on the wedding shower. And it was only *two days* away! How was I going to find a boyfriend by then?

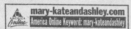

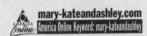